When A Wolf Cries

Mel Dau

B. Love Publications

BLP

Visit bit.ly/readBLP to join our mailing list for sneak peeks and release day links!

Let's connect on social media!
Facebook - B. Love Publications
Twitter - @blovepub
Instagram - @blovepublications

We hate errors, but we are human! If the B. Love team leaves any grammatical errors behind, do us a kindness and send them to us directly in an email to blovepublications@gmail.com **with ERRORS as the subject line.**

As always, if you enjoyed this book, please leave a review on Amazon/Goodreads, recommend it on social media and/or to a friend, and mark it as READ on your Goodreads profile.

By the Book with B Podcast: bit.ly/ bythebookwithb

Come Scootch In

The cries will happen, but always remember to show your teeth.
They bite.

Daddy

My teeth are showing.

Name Pronunciation Key

If there are names/places/things that you find difficult to pronounce or are not sure if your pronunciation is correct, please check here.
Click on the link to hear the pronunciation in the author's voice.

Name/Word
Pronunciation

Elsbeth
    https://voca.ro/1budjDGW9x9z
Darya
    https://voca.ro/11HyogW4Xoef
Rummie
    https://voca.ro/1esHCowHQsmH
Mikayla
    https://voca.ro/1movbZqXi2ka
Parie
    https://voca.ro/1hUAoXpecRYo
Ahote
    https://voca.ro/12LUwNTmK86u
Enola
    https://voca.ro/1j8JSCQOrQBm
Shakina
    https://voca.ro/134IxR2hMHap
Jorie
    https://voca.ro/1g58vL2ZC14T
Chepi
    https://voca.ro/1iEXhmg8BGpO

Prologue

"Dude, act like you at least want to be here, Thad," Farad quipped at his best friend Thaddeus. Farad was frustrated as hell and wanted to be more concerned with the free willing pussy that was roaming around the party ready to get poked.

They were at a hotel party that Farad convinced Thad would be a good time. To Thad, it was anything but. He felt they were too old to be at those types of functions. At thirty-one years old, a lounge or in his house was more his speed. The only reason he came was because the person hosting the party was a college friend. Thad and Farad both attended college together at Winston-Salem State University. They'd been friends since they were babies growing up together.

Thad took a sip from his cup. "If I wanted to be here, I would act like it, Farad. You already know this isn't my speed."

For a hotel ballroom party, it was put together extremely well. There were roped off VIP sections that could be bought with couches. If the VIP was out of your price range, you had the option to buy a table that seated five. Thad and Farad

1

were given a VIP section complimentary from their friend. Good thing because Thad would have never paid $600 to sit in a roped off couch area with only one bottle free. Although he wouldn't, it was clear that many others would and did. The party was packed.

Farad thought the business model was genius. Their friend, Michael, had these parties around North and South Carolina. He worked out a deal with the hotels that would provide the paid ticket holders with a nice discount on a hotel room to discourage drunk driving.

"Aye, my boys! How y'all doing?" Michael came over to speak to his college friends. He'd been busy all night with other party goers to make sure everything was running smoothly.

Thad and Farad stood from their seats to dap him. "Shit, we coolin'. This party is lit as fuck," Farad said.

Michael looked around, proud of his accomplishment. He was excited to see his friends. Farad had been to several of his parties, but this was the first for Thad. He knew this was not his thing. Even in college, Thad was not the type to party. He stayed to himself or he was with Farad. "Thad, how you like the vibe?"

"It's a vibe if you like this kind of thing," he responded. "You know me though. This isn't my thing at all." He wasn't about to lie as if he was enjoying himself. One thing that Thaddeus Patrick Lourie was not was a liar. It wasn't in the nature of who he was as a man.

The only thing that Michael could do was laugh. Thad hadn't changed a bit since college. It was both annoying and refreshing to be around him. "Well, man, you said it was a vibe, just not yours. I'll take that shit."

Thad was happy that he would take that because that was all that he was going to offer. The hairs on the back of his neck rose, putting him on alert. His eyes scanned the room for the source. There were a few reasons that this could have happened, and he was trying to assess why. From wall to wall, he looked. His eyes continued to scan until they stopped at the entrance door. There was a group of girls standing there.

When the DJ shouted out a few of the girls, that piqued Thad's interest even more. "Aye, Michael, who are they?" He pointed toward the girls at the door.

Michael looked toward the direction of his pointed finger. "Oh, that's Kristian, Shakina, and Trice. I'm not sure who the other chick is though," he responded. His eyes tightened. "I don't think I've ever seen her before. She fine as fuck, though, not surprising. Those girls only hang with top quality bitches."

Thad watched the women walk across the room toward a section. He wasn't able to pull his eyes away from this unknown woman. It was like she was calling out to him, but that was impossible... Or was it?

SHE DIDN'T WANT TO BE HERE, BUT SHE DIDN'T WANT TO be in the house alone. When Kristian, Shakina, and Trice reached out to Elsbeth to ask if she wanted to go with them to a party, she hesitantly accepted the invitation. They weren't girls that she'd ever hung out with, but she knew them. Shakina and Elsbeth attended the same high school and now they attended the same college. Elsbeth had obtained a BS in Biology from Shaw University. Now she was studying for her MS in Health-System Pharmacy Administration at the University of North Carolina Chapel Hill (UNC). She was well on her way to being a pharmacist.

"Elsbeth, you gotta loosen up, girl," Shakina commented with a snarky expression. "Here." She handed a drink to Elsbeth. "Drink that and chill the hell out."

I should have stayed my ass in the house like Mikayla told me to. Her best friend, Mikayla or Mi as she called her most of the time, didn't like the group of girls that Elsbeth was currently out with. Shakina was a bitch as far as Mikayla was concerned and she had no idea why all of a sudden, she wanted to be buddy, buddy with her. There was a snake in the grass. The gentle, kind spirit that Elsbeth had was worth protecting.

Elsbeth took the drink and swallowed it in one gulp. She did want to loosen up. There were so many people in the ballroom. The setup was immaculate to say the least. The tickets were one hundred dollars to get in. She was thanking God that she didn't have to pay that because Shakina told her that they had a VIP that was already paid for. "Thank you."

The main buffet in the room was plentiful. She even saw Parker and Lyle, two yays from her past. Yays were what Elsbeth and her best friend called their sneaky links. She'd only had two in her life, and both were here at the same damn time. That sucked like hell, but she wasn't worried. It'd been over five months since she fucked Parker and over a year and a half since she'd messed with Lyle. She hoped neither saw—

Too late. Parker spotted her and had beelined straight to her. He didn't miss Elsbeth per se, but he missed that pretty pussy of hers. She may have been reserved in the streets, but her ass was a slut in the sheets, floor, car, or anywhere else she wanted to fuck. "What's up, Els? Long time no hear from."

She smiled. "Hey, Parker. How are you?"

He admired her beauty. She was the only girl that he'd ever come across with sisterlocks damn near to her ass. "I'm good." He stepped into the section, then took a seat next to her. "I should be asking how are you?"

"I've been good. Busy with work and school. You know me. When I get focused, I stay focused." She held a nonchalant consistency in her tone.

Elsbeth wanted him to move on and enjoy the party. She didn't have anything against him, but she didn't want to deal with him. Three months into dealing with Parker, she found out that he was in a supposedly committed relationship. When she found out, she confirmed before she just walked away. There was no way that she was going to fuss and cuss over a man that wasn't hers. That was idiotic as hell. There was also no need for her to confront him about it because walking away from someone was a full conversation.

Parker's brow peaked. He wasn't sure what her cold demeanor toward him was. The entire time that they fucked with each other there was never any drama between them. "Els, did I do something? It's like one day we were fucking with each other and the next, I couldn't get in touch with you."

Her shoulders lifted to kiss her ears. "That's generally the goal when someone blocks someone. I'm glad to see it worked." Els's body shifted toward him. "Hey, I appreciate you coming to check on me, but it's not necessary. We phased out and that was all that mattered." Her hand went to his leg. "Have a great time tonight."

Parker hated that shit. She was never a woman of many words, but he'd asked her a direct question. He felt disrespected by her because she didn't take the common courtesy to answer him. "Damn, it's like that? You in here trying to ho me like I'm some goofy and I'm just some random ass nigga. That's some real bitch shit."

Elsbeth didn't understand the hostility. "Parker, I'm

confused why you are being hostile right now. How would your fiancée feel about all of this ruckus over little ol' me?"

She had him dead to rights in that moment. His entire soul left his body because he wanted to know how she knew about Asha. Asha lived in Charlotte with their two kids. Yeah, he liked to fuck off from time to time, but he would never leave her. She'd been with him since he was a poor ass corner boy barely able to take care of himself. Now he was making better moves, and he would always make sure she reaped the benefits regardless of what his dick did.

Parker glanced over to Shakina who gave him a knowing look. They were also fucking, but she knew about his fiancée. She simply didn't give a fuck. Shakina also knew that Parker and Elsbeth dealt with each other. Again, she didn't give a flying fuck. If something benefited her, she didn't give a damn about anything else.

"My fiancée don't have shit to do with your ass," he incredulously said. His expression showed that he really believed his stupid ass statement. "What me and you have going on is something separate."

Just as she was about to respond, something caught her eye—or someone. Who in the good heaven's creation of men is that? She'd never seen him before. Well, it wasn't like she would have had many places that she could have seen him. If she wasn't at school, work, or with Mikayla, she was at home. Speaking of Mikayla...

Bestest: Bish, tell those hos I will beat all they asses if they fuk wit u.

Me: lol! No one is fukn with me. Chill. U supposed to be working.

They worked at the same twenty-four-hour pharmacy as pharmaceutical technicians. Tonight, she pulled the short *straw to work the third shift. When Elsbeth told her that she was going with Shakina and her friends to this party, she almost called in sick. It took a lot of convincing for from Elsbeth for her not to.*

Bestest: My ass is working. U know like I do ppl don't come in here this time a night unless it's for a Plan b or condoms.

Me: Well get to condoms and Plan B selling. I'll text you if some crazy shit pops. You got my location.

"Hello!" *Parker's voice broke through her thoughts.*

Her head snapped toward him. "Shit, I forgot you were here. Wait, why are you still here? This conversation is over, hun."

Elsbeth's attention went back to the mystery man that she now noticed was staring at her. His brown-set eyes were enchanting. There was something about him, but she couldn't pinpoint what it was.

"Bitch, fuck you. You really think you're better than the next bitch?" *Parker was confused by his own rage at the situation. Yes, Elsbeth was a beautiful girl. He'd even referred to her as a diamond in the rough.* "Ho, you got me fucked up."

Although Parker's words were forceful, they were not loud, which was a relief. The last thing she wanted was unwanted attention. Once he realized he wasn't going to get anything out of her, Parker stood then left the section. The heat swarmed his body.

"Girl, what was that about? You used to fuck with Parker?" *Shakina's insincere interest in what Elsbeth had going on was a joke. She was the one that told not only Parker but Lyle to come tonight because she was bringing Elsbeth.*

Elsbeth's nose twinkled like she was bewitched before

she set her focus on Shakina. "What that was, was none of your business. What's even more, none of your business is my pussy matters."

Shakina's body stiffened for a second to the cold, stern words of Elsbeth. That reaction from her was unexpected since she usually was a more kindred spirit. On a normal day, Shakina would have snapped, but that day, there was an objective at hand. She swallowed her pride and desire to slap the shit out of Elsbeth.

"I didn't mean anything by it," Shakina said with her best deep smile that she could muster. "You're right. I need to mind the business that pays me. Your pussy doesn't make me a dime." She giggled.

Elsbeth's attention went back to mystery man, who was still gawking at her. Should I wave, smile, or just ignore him? She went with her first mind. The corner of her lips rose, and her hand demurely waved.

"Y'all asses going to sit down all night or have some fun, bitches?" Trice came over with two drinks in her hand. She extended the cups out to Shakina and Elsbeth. "Drink, bitches!"

They both took the cups. Shakina drank hers in one gulp while Elsbeth was still in a trance, staring at mystery man. Shakina tapped the bottom of Elsbeth's cup with silent instruction to take the drink. Just as she was about to take the drink to the head, the sexy mystery man gave her a head nod before a salute.

―――――――――

"DAMN, YOU GONNA EAT THE GIRL'S PUSSY FROM HERE?" Farad joked with Thad. "What she smell like, nigga?"

Thad's attention didn't shift from the beauty as he closed

out all the scents in the room to isolate hers. "She smells like lilac, almond, and a hint of rose."

Her scent was arousing to his senses. This was something that he never experienced. Farad stopped smiling and laughing. He knew the severity of a wolf being able to isolate the scent of a woman, especially when she wasn't a fellow wolf. Farad didn't need a crystal ball to know what was coming next.

"Thaddeus, I don't have time for your crazy shit. I got too much shit to be doing." Farad knew that his best friend could be with the shit when provoked.

Thaddeus being with the shits in human form was a tornado. Him being with the shits as a wolf was a tornado that caused an earthquake. Farad had never witnessed Thad going ape shit over a female, but he'd also never seen him liking any female on a deeper level than pussy and an occasional trip to Waffle House.

"I need to find out who she is." Thad spoke to himself more than Farad.

When he and Farad walked into the party, they didn't need to look around to know that members of their pack were in the room. Both were members of the Lumbee Tribe in Lumberton, North Carolina. Thad was the leader of the pack and Farad was his second in command. Being the leader of a pack was a lot of responsibility, especially when your father was the chief. Heavy was the head that wore the crown.

Thaddeus opened his mind to speak telepathically to the pack. "Aye, do any of you know the chick sitting on the couch to the right of my section with those other three girls? She has the locs."

There was a moment as the pack narrowed in on who their leader referred to. Jorie spoke up. "I don't know her name, but she works at that twenty-four-hour pharmacy near UNC. She goes to UNC too."

That would make sense that Jorie knew that because she was a student there as well. "You know anything about her?" Thad asked Jorie.

"Not really. When I see her on campus, she's by herself or with some other girl." Jorie paused for a second. "I've never seen her with those girls though. Surprised she's with them bitches honestly."

He didn't know anything about the other females any more than he knew about the mystery girl that was possessing his thoughts. "Something is off about them. Everyone keep eyes on her."

They all agreed before he closed his mind back. The party continued to flow on through the night. Thad watched as the women fed his beauty drinks after drinks. That was weird activity to him. He caught her more than a few times, glancing his way.

The party was slated to end around three in the morning. Around one, Thad watched the four girls leave the room. That wouldn't have struck him as odd, if it didn't appear like his beauty was far more drunk than the other girls when they all had been downing drink after drinks together. He was going to give them ten minutes to come back before he went to find her.

Farad had been observing the scene like his best friend asked. "Aye, you see that shit?" Farad's shoulder bumped Thad's from where he sat next to him.

He saw exactly what Farad saw. Whoever the dude was that sat next to his beauty earlier in the night left the room with four other niggas. When he was sitting with her earlier, they looked like they weren't having the greatest conversation. Thaddeus opened his mind.

"Someone follow those niggas that are walking out," he instructed. He was on his feet heading toward the door himself.

Four members of the pack immediately headed out of the room. His beast started to wake up. That was never a good thing in situations like those.

"Aye, y'all leaving already?" Michael stopped them just as they were about to leave the room. He had a drink in his hand and a bitch on his arm.

Farad stepped forward. "Yeah, man, we're heading out. This was lit though." He dapped Michael. "Let us know when you have another one."

Seconds later, they were leaving the ballroom. Thad was locked into his pack telepathically, so he'd know where to go. They weren't saying anything just yet.

"I found them," Oscar announced to the pack. "They went to the eighteen floor, room 1825. Do you want us to stay out here until you get here?"

Thad told him that he did. It wouldn't take him long to assess the room once he got there. Luckily, the elevator had just reached the main floor when they arrived. Farad used his keycard to activate it. He'd gotten a room in anticipation of getting some pussy. It took less than a minute for the elevator doors to open at the eighteenth floor. They moved down the hall toward the direction of the room.

"What's up, Thad?" Oscar dapped him and Farad. "I'm not sure what's going on in there, but I heard females in there too."

Thad moved to the door of the suite and stood in front of it. His brown eyes glistened over before gray specks appeared. The gods saw fit to bless him with the gift of x-ray vision. "Farad."

"I'm already on it," he said as he took his place next to his

11

best friend. As if their friendship was ordained by the gods, he was gifted with sonar hearing.

The wall disappeared from Thad's sight, giving him clear sight. There were way too many people in the single king bed hotel room. He saw the three girls and the five guys but didn't see his beauty. He opened his senses and smelled her, so he knew she was there.

"What are they saying?" he asked Farad.

Farad was silent. He was taking in the conversation and was in a state of disbelief. The words were on the tip of his tongue, but they were stopped when Thad's hand gripped his arm tightly.

"She's on the bed passed out. They took her fucking clothes off." He didn't know what the hell was going on, but it couldn't be good.

Farad looked at his best friend. "They're talking about fucking her and shit. The girls are telling the dudes that she won't remember because they put something in her drink." He shook his head. "Muthafuckas are sick."

Thaddeus took a step back as he looked between the pack members that were in the hallway with him. Four were already there and three more were on the way based on the group telepathic conversations happening. Here, tonight, only two of the female pack members, Jorie and Maggie, were at the party.

He pulled the gun that was secured behind him to check it. The other three pack members came into the hallway. "Y'all know how I do," Thad said to everyone. "No shifting."

Thad handed his room key to Jorie before he told her, Maggie, and Oscar to get his beauty when they got in there and take her to his room. "Bro, we need to hurry up. It sounds like one of those niggas are ready to start the sick party."

"Say less," Thad said. He moved back to where he stood

in front of the door. He heard guns clicking behind him letting him know that his pack was ready for whatever. "Let's get my beauty."

His leg lifted, then his foot went to the door. One kick was all he needed for the door to bust open off its hinges. Everyone in the room jumped. Guns were drawn by two of the men in the room. They were a little too late to the draw because Oscar and Cecil had delivered a silent shot to their hands disarming them.

The girls screamed, ran to the corner, and covered. They looked terrified like they just hadn't committed the most heinous of sins. Shady bitches were interesting.

"Shut the fuck up with all that bitch shit. Y'all asses wasn't screaming when you were setting this girl up to be raped with your stupid asses!" Thad roared. His attention turned to Parker. "So, you and ya boys like raping women?"

Parker's hands flew up." Nah, nah, it wasn't no shit like that. I was telling them that this shit was foul," he lied. He talked a lot of shit, but he was half of what he claimed. Yeah, he'd moved up in the streets, but he was still very much a do boy. Parker was able to fool many because they didn't have direct access to who was really in charge.

Farad stepped forward, then said, "A lie don't care who fucking tell it." He turned to Thad. "How do you want to handle this?"

Jorie grabbed the extra comforter from the closet to cover Elsbeth's naked body. After she was covered, Oscar lifted her from the bed. Her head dropped back like she was dead, causing Thaddeus's heart to tighten. This is her. She belongs to me.

He opened his mind to his sister Rumble who everyone called Rummie. "Sis, I need you now."

Rummie was a registered nurse who had a bachelor's in nursing science. "What's wrong, Thad? Where are you?"

Thad and Rummie were tremendously close only being sixteen months apart. "Track me. When you pin me come to room 1512."

Relative and mates can track each other. Pack leaders can track the members of their packs when necessary and be tracked if desired. The gods gave wolves many gifts that differ per wolf. Thad and Rummie's second cousins had the gift of being mixed breeds because of their grandmother's blood. Some of them were able to shift into not only wolves but centaurs. They lived on the west coast though.

"I got you. I'll be there soon. Can I shift to get there faster or drive?" It was customary for members of the pack to ask permission to shift it they weren't hunting.

He thought about it. "Drive. I may need you to transport someone." After he and his sister concluded their conversation, he looked at his best friend. "I'm more concerned with my beauty. Something tells me that they may have learned their lessons."

"Yes, yes, please," Shakina blurted. She'd never regretted anything more than she regretted trying to set Elsbeth up. "We won't tell anyone. We swear."

Shakina hated Elsbeth. It had nothing to do with anything that Elsbeth did. It had more to do with who Shakina wasn't. Since high school, she'd always hated that Elsbeth didn't have to try to be beautiful. While Shakina had to make sure every hair was in place, clothes designer, and makeup perfectly applied for niggas to even give her half of a second glance. She was far from an ugly female, however, being a mean girl could take a toll on how others saw you.

Elsbeth could come to school in sweats, dirty ass skateboard sneakers, face absent of any makeup except lip gloss, and her hair in a scrunchie. Niggas would still fall all over her as if she was the second coming of Mary. God blessed her with perfect eyebrows and long lashes that Shakina had to pay for. While Shakina wore three-thousand-dollar weaves, Elsbeth had sisterlocked hair down her back.

When they ended up going to school together again, there was so much unnecessary resentment in Shakina's heart toward her. It didn't make it any better when she found out from Parker directly that he was fucking with Elsbeth. Parker had been fucking with Shakina off and on since they were in high school. He never took her seriously and it showed when he refused to let his girlfriend, now fiancée go at her request. She tried to make the request of him again when they started messing around again, but he refused. To add insult to injury, he said he'd leave his girl for Elsbeth before he ever left his fiancée for Shakina.

That was when she came up with this plan. Her goal was to convince the guys to fuck Elsbeth and she would tape it. She would use the tape to embarrass Elsbeth after convincing her that she was a willing participant as well as cause turmoil in Parker's relationship. It was easy to convince Kristian and Trice to go along with the plan. They'd do anything to stay on Shakina's ass.

Thad stepped in front of the women, then squatted down. "I'm not worried about anyone in this room saying shit. Just remember, there are things that are far worse than death." He reached his hand out and touched each woman's cheek. "I'll be watching."

He stood after he gave them a flirtatious wink. His eyes roamed the room at the men who were there like bitches. The two that were shot cried on the ground, holding their hands. "You gentlemen have a good night."

He strolled out of the room as if he and his pack hadn't

caused a quick scene of chaos. The second his foot crossed the threshold into the hallway, he knew that he would do anything for this woman that he didn't even know her name. There was something about his beauty that had him stuck. At this point he had no plan to become unstuck. The question was whether she'd be as willing to get stuck to him.

Elsbeth "Els" Darya Sanders

Oh God! Why is my head pounding? My hand went to my head, trying to remember anything from last night. I was drawing a blank which wasn't a good thing. All I could remember was going out with Shakina, Kristian, and Trice to a party. Drinks were drunk and some fun was had, but from there, I was lost. My eyes slowly opened but closed abruptly to the brightness of the room.

After another minute or so, I slowly opened them again, letting them adjust. Once they were open, panic set in. *Why am I in a hotel room?* I looked under the comforter, and I was completely naked. *Oh God, what did I do?"*

"Calm down, Elsbeth. You're all right," a female voice said from the side of me. "Take a deep breath."

My head snapped in the direction of the voice. I sat up in the bed putting my back on the headboard. I made sure to keep my body covered with the comforter. "What's going on? Who are you?"

There were two other females in the room that I didn't know. *Was I being trafficked?* I was very traffickable.

"My name is Rumble, but everyone calls me Rummie. This is Maggie and Jorie," she said as she pointed to the other females in the room. She stepped closer to me, then stopped. She doubled back, grabbed something off a nearby table, then started her trek toward me again. "Here's your purse. I had to go into it to find your name. Am I pronouncing it correctly?"

I nodded my head more, impressed than I wanted to be after she repeated my name. Almost everyone fucked up my name, if they even tried. Most resorted to calling me Beth, which I abhorred. "Great! We all know each other," I said with tight eyes. "Is anyone able to explain why I'm naked in a hotel room with three chicks that I don't know?"

The girl named Rummie pulled a chair close to the bed. Her sullen expression told me that I wouldn't like whatever she was about to tell me. I sat there in silence while she told me about the events of last night. My heart ached at the news that the only reason I was invited out by Shakina was for her to set me up to be raped. At some point I must have zoned out because I didn't feel Rummie sit next to me until her arm wrapped around me. I wanted to push her away, but I needed someone right now. I fell into her arms with tears streaming down my cheeks.

How could someone hate someone that much to set them up to be sexually assaulted? When she said that Parker was involved, I wanted to throw up. I should have listened to Mikayla. *Mikayla!* My head popped up. "I have to call my best friend."

I grabbed my purse that sat beside me and fumbled through it to find my phone. I grabbed it, then long held the number two on the screen. I held my breath until she picked up after the second ring.

"Bitch, where the fuck are you? I've been calling you all

night. I know your ass is at the hotel. I'm on the eleventh floor knocking on these fuckas doors looking for you," she rambled. *"Those fuckas downstairs told me that I couldn't come upstairs if I wasn't a guest. They had me fucked up. I swiped the maid's card and if these fuckas didn't answer after I knocked, I was coming in."* Her breathing was hard.

I wasn't sure where I was to give her an answer. My gaze went to Rummie. "What room is this?"

"Who are you with? Why are you asking them where you are?" Mikayla rushed out. *"You should know where the hell you are, Els!"*

Rummie told me that I was in room 1512 and I relayed that information to her. She told me she was on her way before she hung up the line. My heartbeat slowed knowing that she was in the building.

"I love how your best friend cuts for you. That's important," Jorie said cheerfully. Her smile was bright.

My smile was small, but it was there. "Yeah, I love her. I wished I listened to her and didn't go out with those bitches last night."

Mikayla must have run up the stairs or something because seconds later she was banging on the door. Rummie rushed to the door to answer. The door wasn't opened completely before my bestest pushed it open. "Where is she?"

Her eyes were wide as they scanned the room. It didn't take long for her to find me and rush over to me. She touched all over me and questioned me about what happened. My emotional dam broke again at her concern for me. I wanted to tell her what happened, but how could I? Rummie stepped up to tell her what happened. Mikayla's tears flowed as freely as mine.

Mikayla's face was tight. "I'm going to kill that fucking

bitch! Oh, and Parker wants to play the rape game? I got something special for his bitch ass!"

I knew she meant everything that she said because she reminded me almost daily that she did not play about me. Her hold on me was tight. Any tighter, she might have broken me.

I cleared my throat the best I could to speak. "Thank you for helping me. I don't know what I would have done if you didn't come along."

Rummie was looking at her phone. Her head popped up with her focus on me. "Oh, you can thank my brother for that. He's actually on his way up in the elevator now with his best friend and our mom. I told him that it would be best if only females were in the room when you woke up."

We sat in silence for a minute before there was a soft knock at the door. Once again, Rummie stood to get the door. My breath got caught in my throat when the mystery man that I eye stalked last night walked into the room. The darkness of the room last night did him no justice. He was breathtakingly handsome. When his eyes landed on me, it felt like my skin was heated.

"Hey, Elsbeth, how are you feeling?" His voice had a melodic undertone that was soothing. It could lull you to sleep or keep you awake. It would just depend on the conversation.

My head tilted and my shoulders lifted. "As well as a girl can who was set up to be raped." Hearing myself say the sentence was sickening. "Thank you for saving me."

"No thank you needed, Beauty. I thank the gods that I was in the building to intercept those fuck niggas. My name is Thaddeus, by the way. Everyone calls me Thad." His smile was sincere and beautiful.

Mikayla jumped up from the bed, ran to Thad, and

wrapped her arms around his neck with tears in her eyes. "Thank you so much for saving my best friend! I don't know what I would have done if those fuck niggas and bitches hurt her."

He wrapped his arms around her waist. "Again, no thanks. Farad and I were at the right place at the right time to make sure shit didn't happen to her."

Mikayla moved to who he referred to as Farad and threw her arms around his neck to thank him. His smile said loud and clear that he appreciated her hug. *I guess I know who she's going to be fucking soon.*

"Rumble, did you check her out?" an older woman asked. "Oh, I'm sorry, baby. I'm Parie, Rumble and Thaddeus's mother." She held up a bag that I just noticed she was holding. "When my baby boy told me what happened, I insisted on coming. I'm a doctor and Rumble is a nurse."

I thought it was adorable that she referred to her son as baby boy. From the annoyed expression on her baby boy's face, he didn't agree. Her daughter let her know that she did check me out.

"Okay, good. Here, baby, I got you some clothes. They might be too big, but I know you need some." Parie extended a bag to me.

I took the bag. "Thank you, Mrs. Parie. I'm sure whatever you got was fine." I moved around on the bed sure that I held the cover firmly. "Mikayla, can you help me in the bathroom?"

She rushed to my side. Her hand held the comforter firmly around me. "Come on, Bestest."

Everyone stepped back to give us room. I felt like a spectacle as we walked into the bathroom. The second the door closed behind us my body collapsed to the ground. My hand covered my face. "Why would they do this to me? I don't bother anyone, Mi!"

She dropped next to me, pulled me in her arms, and rocked me. "I know you don't, I know. Some people are just hateful, but don't worry. You know I fuck bitches up for shits and giggles."

I didn't want to laugh, but I couldn't help it. That was her favorite saying and it always pulled a laugh from me in any situation. Rummie knocked lightly. She let me know that everything I needed to take a shower was in here. That's when I noticed the bag of hygiene items on the counter.

I'm sure we were in the bathroom longer than anticipated. I needed time to get myself together for many different reasons. The trauma of what happened although I had no memory of it was heavy. My spirit was also conflicted because of the mystery man who I now know as Thaddeus was the one who saved me from something that could have ruined my existence.

After I was dressed, we exited the bathroom. I noticed the only people left in the room were Rummie, Thad, and Mrs. Parie. I sat down in the open chair that was available. Rummie encouraged me to eat some of the food that sat on the table, so I did.

"Hey, if you don't mind, can we exchange numbers? I want to just check on you from time to time," Rummie asked with sympathy. "Maybe we can go to brunch or something."

For a beat, I thought about it. I peeked at Mikayla who nodded her approval. After last night, I planned to consult with my bestest about everyone. She had this knack for reading people. My mama told me that she had the spirit of discernment. "I would like that."

We exchanged numbers quickly before I told them that I was going to leave. I thanked Rummie, Thad, and Mrs. Parie. They didn't have to do everything that they did. Mi and I walked out into the hallway hand in hand. Before we got too far, Thad called out to me.

His walk resembled a person walking on a cloud. He wore a casual sweatsuit with sneakers that complemented it. His scent invaded my senses the closer he got to me. "Hey, if you need anything, I don't care how big or small, please don't hesitate to reach out to my sister. Whatever she can't do, I will."

My words were caught... somewhere. I wasn't sure where they were, but I knew that I couldn't find them. My hand squeezed Mi's hand. I needed her to speak for me. The problem with that was, I could never be sure what her wildcard ass would say.

"She sure will. I will make sure of it." The glee in her voice made me want to pinch her. "Thank you again."

He smiled, touched my shoulder, then turned on his heel. His touch had my insides melting. I couldn't take my stare off him as he walked away. Mi and I didn't start back down the hall until we heard the room door close. I gave Mi a serious side-eye when we got to the elevator.

"Bitch, don't look at me. Yes, if you need something I'm texting Rummie immediately to tell her fine ass brother," she snapped. "That could be your baby daddy, your husband, or both."

All I could do was snicker. "Girl, take me to my mama and daddy's house. I saw my mama called me a few times too."

Harry and Marci Sanders were my life, and I was theirs. Since I was born, they treated me like a porcelain doll. A lot of that had to do with me being their rainbow baby after multiple miscarriages. My mom told me that for my first three years of life, I slept in their room because she was so terrified that I would die in my sleep. Marci was my ultimate best friend and Harry was my ultimate protector.

My parents lived twenty minutes away from the hotel. I was told by them that I never had to call before I came. They gave me a key, but I still knocked before I came into their house. Their old asses still liked to have sex around the house. I gagged at the thought of it. I loved the house I grew up in. Over the years, it changed a lot, but the homey feeling never left.

I rang the doorbell camera and waited for my mama to tell me to come in. It didn't take long for her to unlock the door, but not before she voiced her annoyance with me. Mi and I both chuckled at her country ass. Like I knew she would be, she was in the kitchen. For Christmas last year, I bought her an indoor herb garden. Since she received it, she'd purchased three more. Now she only cooked with fresh herbs.

Marci was the most beautiful woman in my eyes, and I was blessed to look like she spit me out. She played with her herbs for a few more seconds before she looked up with a smile. As soon as her eyes contacted mine, her smile faltered. "What's wrong? Mi, what happened to her?"

A part of me wanted to be bothered that she knew something was wrong with me just from a look. The other part thanked God for my mother's empathic spirit. Mi and I sat at the kitchen nook. My mother immediately started to brew tea. There would be no talking until it was steeped. It didn't take long for it to steep thank God. She'd set out everything we needed to enjoy it.

After the tea was poured, she sat. "Tell me what's going on. Don't lie to me either. You know I'll know, lil girl."

It felt like this would be the hardest thing that I'd ever have to do. With a deep intake of breath, I rambled out what happened to me. My mother sat frozen with an unreadable expression. Mi and I, on the other hand, were in a fit of tears. After I finished, she still sat there with no words.

"What y'all in here talking about?" My father's voice startled me. I hadn't heard him come into the house. He wasn't home when we arrived. "Who done had a baby or something that got y'all crying?"

He tittered, then moved to my mother to kiss her cheek. It wasn't until after he kissed her cheek that he felt the true heaviness of the room. My mother still had yet to move or say anything. My father abruptly went into protector mode. "What the fuck is going on?"

Robotically, my mother repeated the story that I told her. My father stood there and listened with his arms across his chest and his stance wide. After she was done, he nodded his head and walked out of the room. I didn't know what to think. My mother reached out, grabbed my hand, then squeezed it. Seconds later, my head turned to the sound of footsteps.

"Daddy, what are you doing?" The pitch of my voice elevated. "Why do you have those?"

He walked back into the kitchen with a sawed-off shotgun that I didn't know he owned and a Glock. My father was a retired sheriff who still taught firearm classes and safety.

He gazed at me lovingly before he cupped my cheek with his hand. "Baby, your daddy is about to go hunting. Don't worry. Daddy is going to take care of it." He shifted his body toward Mikayla. "Mi-Mi, what's the nigga's name that I need to practice my new taxidermy hobby on?"

My mind tried desperately to speak to Mi's mind to not

tell him as if that was a thing. Well, it didn't work. The smirk on her face told me she was about to tell all of the business with high enthusiasm.

"Oh, Pop Harry, his name is Parker. He had four of his homeboys with him," she answered. She tapped my shoulder. "Wait, Rummie said that Thaddeus shot two of them in the hand."

My father shifted on his feet. His face scrunched. "Who is Rummie and Thaddeus?"

Finally, my voice decided to rejoin the conversation. "Thaddeus was the guy that saw what was going on in the party. When they took me out of the party room, he became suspicious. He saved me and took me to another room where his sister, who's a nurse, tended to me."

My daddy pulled out the notepad that he kept in the back of his pocket, then grabbed the pen that was on the table. He flipped the notepad open. "What's those names again?" I repeated them and he wrote them down. "Thanks, baby girl. Marci, baby, make sure we invite them to dinner."

"I sure will, baby. Mi and Els, make sure you find out what they like to eat. Dinner is next Sunday." My mother had spoken. There was no need to pushback when it came to Marci Sanders. Under God, then my daddy, her word was law.

I let a low huff. "Okay, Mama, I will." My body turned to my daddy. "Daddy, I don't want you to go hunting. He's going to get handled."

"Damn right that fuck boy is gonna be handled and so is that bitch Shakina," Mi blurted. She slapped her hand over her mouth with wide eyes. "I'm sorry, Ma Marci and Pop Harry."

She never cursed around my parents. I wanted to roar in laughter at the fear in her eyes, like my mother was going to hop across the table and spank her. Now when we were younger, my mother had put hands on her. Both of us went through a rebellious stage around eighth grade that required stern words and swift hands.

"Lil baby, I'm going to give you a pass today. Your description of them is spot on." My mama was trying to hold in her laughter.

After a little more convincing, my daddy agreed to not go hunting yet. He made sure to point out that the operative word was yet. My mother cooked us all lunch and we sat around to talk more. My daddy didn't speak much, but he made Mi move seats so he could sit next to me. It was almost like he wanted to make up for not protecting me last night by sitting close to me now. My daddy was my superhero. There was nothing in the world that would ever change that.

A Few Days Later...

"I'm so ready to get my ass home and in my bed," I whined. I was exhausted after having class this morning then working a shift in the pharmacy. "Bitch, where are we going?"

Mi and I had classes and worked our shifts together today, so she decided to drive. Our apartments were next door to each other. Originally, I wanted us to live together, but my best friend loved her own space. She suffered traumas from her childhood and teenage years. She grew up in the foster care system jumping around until she was adopted when she was eight years old. Shortly after, her and her parents moved here to Raleigh, North Carolina.

Her parents never physically abused her, but they were not nice people. They deprived her of things that people should never be deprived of. She spent a lot of time at my house after we became friends. It became clear early in our sleepovers that one of the things that she was deprived of was food. The following morning after the first night she slept over, my mother cleaned my room and found food that she was hoarding.

My family did everything to make her feel safe. Unfortunately, some of her trauma followed her into adulthood. One of those things being having her own separate space from everyone to keep her possessions safe.

"I know you heard me ask you a question, Mikayla," I said with more aggression.

She glanced at me, then said, "I'm going to beat a bitch's ass. You can join or watch. Whatever works best for you."

My eyelids expanded. "What the hell are you talking about? Mi, I know you didn't..."

My words faded when we pulled up to a house I'd never seen. Mi turned off the car and jumped out before I could say another word. I rushed to follow her. She was on the porch before I could get to her. "Where are we?" I asked.

She nonchalantly responded, "We're at Shakina's house. Luckily, she's a customer at the pharmacy." Her hand went to her hip. "Did you know that bitch has herpes? Don't tell anyone. Wouldn't want to violate HIPAA."

"We should not be here. Do you know how much trouble we'd be in if she called the police?" My best friend was crazy as hell. She was always on go and never minded fucking a bitch up. I'm not saying that I would never fuck a bitch up because I was just as much with the shit. I just took more time to think about the actions before I made a move.

Mikayla was a fuck you up then rationalize why you had to be fucked up later type.

"Girl, shut up. This bitch set you up to be raped and you're worried about the cops." The disgust was real in her tone. I knew she meant no harm, but the words still hurt my feelings. She reached out for the knob, then turned it. "Just like a dumb bitch to leave her door unlocked. That's so unsafe of her."

Mi walked into her house like it was hers. It wasn't a very big house. It was one of those single family, patio homes. I followed my best friend as she walked down the short hallway. Only one door in the hallway was closed. She turned to me, then in a low voice said, "Behind this door a whore lies. Pun intended."

She opened the door slowly. We both stepped in. "Well, ain't this about a bitch."

There was Shakina, the girl who set me up to be raped, and Parker, the guy who was willing to rape me, in the bed cozy and asleep. Rage overwhelmed me. I didn't feel myself jump on this bitch's head, but I was sure that she did.

"Ah!" Shakina screamed as my fist punched her unsuspected face. "Stop, stop, stop!"

A part of me felt bad because I wasn't a person who liked to sneak attack people. This situation was an extenuating circumstance in my opinion. I'll forgive myself later. "Bitch, you set me up to be fucking raped!"

Parker didn't have time to react because Mikayla was on his ass. It wasn't a surprise that Shakina couldn't fight. *Wait, I didn't give her a chance to fight.* I got off of her, then stepped back. "Let me give you a chance for a fair one, bitch."

Shakina didn't ask why I was there. That much should have been obvious I would think. It took her a second to get her bearings before she charged at me. Shakina was bigger than me, so I knew she would use her weight. Smart fighting strategy, but I was quicker. I kicked her right in her hungry ass knee, and she dropped. She bellowed in pain. A quick two piece and a slap had her laid out.

My attention refocused on what was going on with Mi and Parker. She was tearing him up mostly because he didn't seem to want to hit her. The way she tagged him, if I were him, I would have laid her out. When he started to overpower her, I ran over to help. A kick to the dick had him crippled on the ground.

"You're a bitch and I hate you!" I shouted. "Does your fiancée know you're a rapist? Huh, does she?" My tears dropped on him as I kicked him repeatedly.

He was not only going to rape me, but let his sick homeboys have a try. His sexual relationship with Shakina didn't bother me. I didn't have any vested feelings for him; therefore, where he stuck his dick was his prerogative. The reason I stopped our situationship had nothing to do with feelings. It had everything to do with principle and morality. If I were in a relationship, I wouldn't want anyone fucking my man.

A final kick in his face made me feel better. He groaned loudly. I left him and his accomplice on the floor. There was nothing more for me to do here. I got to Mi's car before she did. I sat there wondering why she didn't come out right after me. Just as I was about to get back out of the car she came bopping out of the house with a psychotic smile.

"Didn't that feel amazing?" she asked when she got into the car. "I love beating a bitch up midday. Best cardio ever." She held her arm up in my face. I wasn't sure what I was looking at. "Look how high my heart rate got."

I was not about to play with her. "Take me home. I just don't know why you're like this."

"You said take you home hard like we don't live next damn door to each other," she said after she cut her eye in my direction. "Okay, I'll take us home."

She pulled out of Shakina's driveway. She made the choice that we needed to go grocery shopping before we went home. That always baffled me. We didn't live together but she always ate at my house. She bought groceries for her apartment, but most of the groceries went to mine. "Aye, did you text Rummie to let her know about dinner Sunday?"

I would argue, but why? I've always told Mikayla that she should be a damn lawyer. She was the captain of the debate team in high school and undergrad. I pulled out my phone. "I'm doing it right now."

Me: Hi, Rummie. This is Elsbeth. My mama wanted to invite U, Thaddeus and Farad over for dinner on Sunday. Is that ok?

Rummie had texted me over the past few days to check on me. I always answered but kept the conversation short. I didn't really know what to say to her.

Rummie: Hey girlie! That would be amazing. Just let me know the details.

Me: Is there anything that any of you don't eat or are allergic to?

Rummie: Nope! We're all pretty much carnivores.

Me: Ok. I'll let my mama know. I'll send you the time and address soon.

"It's done," I told Mi. *She gets on my nerves.* I wasn't looking forward to Sunday, but in the same breath, I was.

31

Thaddeus "Thad" Patrick Lourie

A Day Later...

"So, you been casually stalking this girl's social media?" Farad guffawed at my expense. "This is worse than I thought it was. A little crush this is not."

He was right. This was way more than some little crush. I knew nothing about this damn girl except what she posted on social media. She didn't post a lot, but it was enough to learn what I needed about her. The thing that stood out the most about her was her love for mythology. She had video after video on her page about different gods and goddesses. I watched every single one of them, liked them, and went a step further to put hearts in the comments.

I had to go through those comments to see if there were any niggas I needed to kill, I mean look out for. The only reason I started a social media page was to see her page. That's why Farad thought all of this was so funny. "Man, shut up. Elsbeth is going to be my mate when the time is right."

Farad's laughter quickly ceased. *Yeah, I just said that wolf trigger word.* "Man, you for real right now? You want her to be your mate?"

"That's what I said." I took a pull from my blunt. "You know I don't say shit just to hear myself talk."

We were at my house on the reservation. I loved my house that was gifted to me on my twenty-first birthday. My sister was also gifted with a house. Both of our homes were built for a full family. All the wolf parents that I know advocate for their children to mate as soon as they turn twenty. My parents were no different. Patrick and Parie were chomping at the bit for me to mate and give them grandchildren.

When I turned thirty and still hadn't mated, I thought my father would have an aneurysm. His thought process was that the Chief's son should already be married and mated. Be clear that those two things were not synonymous. My father even went as far as to ask me whether I was a homosexual. That was a damn joke.

"Thad, you do know that shit is going to be halfway impossible. You know your dad wants his line pure," Farad pointed out. "You willing to go through all that shit for her?"

Once again, my best friend had a point. Both of my parents were wolves, and my father wanted to keep our line one hundred percent pure. I never really cared or thought about the whole keep the line pure thing because I never wanted to mate with anyone. Yeah, I'd been in relationships in the past but nothing serious and yes, they were with wolves. That mostly was out of convenience.

I thought about everything that Farad asked. "Yeah, for Elsbeth, I am. I'd walk through the valley to visit hell, redecorate that ho into my own heaven to be with her. Nothing is going to stop me from being with that woman."

Farad looked off toward the window in the direction of my parents' home, then back at me. "I hope you mean that, brother. Fucking with your dad, hell might be what you get." He took a hit from the blunt that was in his hand. "You know I ride with you at every dawn, noon, and night."

My phone vibrated on the table. I looked at it to see a preview of my sister's text on the screen. I picked it up to read it.

Rummie: Hey! Elsbeth's parents invited me, you and Farad to dinner on Sunday at 7 pm. Meet me at my house at 6:15 and we'll all ride together.

Me: Oh ok. I guess I'm going to dinner.

Rummie: lol! No guess, you are. Kisses!

"Bro, we're having dinner with Elsbeth's parents on Sunday," I said with a titter.

Farad snickered. "The gods are working in your favor I see. I heard your ass changed your route."

Both of us were United States Postal Service (USPS) workers and had been for over six years. When people found out about our careers, they looked at us like we were lames. This job was by choice and not necessity. The Lourie family had been the leaders of the Lumbee tribe for generations. Money was not a problem, especially with the casino that we owned. My dad's cousin that lived in Washington State helped our tribe establish it and it's one of the highest earning casinos in the state. If you add on the hotel and restaurant, my family had money.

I decided to work as a USPS worker because honestly it was something to do outside of the tribe. People in the tribe asked why I didn't just start a business instead of working for someone else. Yeah, that was all fine and dandy, but when you own a business, you're thinking about the success of that business all the time. I wanted to go to work, do my job, then leave work at work. There were some people who are fine with working for others and not being the boss in that arena.

"Yeah, I did change my route to add the pharmacy that Elsbeth works at and her apartment complex." I shrugged, then tilted my head toward my shoulder. "You know I have to stay close to my mate."

Farad smiled. "I'm guessing that you somehow got her work schedule to make sure that the mail is delivered at a time when she was at work." He knew me so well.

"Why you asking questions that you know the answer to?" I shook my head. "She works tomorrow, so I'll see her tomorrow."

I needed to implant myself into her life. The hearts and likes on her posts were not enough. Although, I knew she saw them and was lurking on my page. She accidentally liked a post from over a year ago. She pulled the like back, but not before I got the notification. We'd see how that plan went tomorrow.

The Next Day...

I was appreciative that it was a nice day today. As a wolf, it was rare that we got hot in our human form when we weren't transforming. When I worked, I spent most of my time in my truck except when I delivered to businesses. I ironically was a social person when it came to my job. In my personal life, I couldn't say the same thing.

The pharmacy that Elsbeth worked at was not a new

business, but they had recently moved to a newer retail and restaurant area. There were retail stores and restaurants at the bottom of new condominiums that were built. Based on Els's address, she lived a few blocks from the pharmacy. In the state of North Carolina, the law states that all mailboxes at apartment complexes had to be centralized. Her complex had seventy-five units with a ninety-eight percent capacity. That would take me roughly an hour and a half to two hours to finish distribution of the mail.

Like the strategic planner that I am, I plan to schedule that distribution around the time that my mate gets off. I realized that meant that people wouldn't get their mail at the same time every day, but I didn't give a fuck. I knew my baby picked her mail up after she came home from work.

I was two stores away from seeing my baby in her element. Last night, I sent her a reel on TikTok with this nigga talking about how he would be loyal and love his girl. An hour later, she sent me back a reel from a female point of view that expressed the same sentiment. *Yeah, she likes a nigga.*

When I got to the pharmacy, I looked down at my uniform to make sure I was well put together. There was no reason for me to look because I was always together. Before I walked in, I took the mail out. The pharmacy was a small, black, family-owned business. The pharmacist was the owner and who I gave the mail to. This would be the first time that I delivered the mail, so that gave me the opportunity to introduce myself.

The cashier was the first person to notice me. Her eyes glossed over. That reaction was common. "Hey! Are you our new mailman?" She cooed with her words as her eyelashes threatened to fly her away.

"Yes, ma'am, I am. My name is Thaddeus, but you can

call me Thad. It's my pleasure to meet you." I gave her my hand to shake.

She grabbed it tightly. "No, it is all my pleasure, trust me. I hope I'm working every time you deliver the mail. My name is Amanda." She brazenly flirted.

"We'll just have to see, Amanda," I said before I winked.

Her cheeks brightened. I turned on my heels to make my way to the back section of the store where the pharmacy was. I saw Els before she saw me. *Fuck, she's gorgeous.* I assumed she was filling a prescription.

When the pharmacist, Mr. Bill, looked up, he smiled at my presence. "Hey, man! Rudy told me yesterday was his last day on this route." Mr. Bill came from behind the counter. "I'm Mr. Bill, the owner and pharmacist."

I took the hand that he extended to shake. "Aye, man. I'm Thaddeus or Thad. Yes, Mr. Rudy wanted a smaller route so he could spend more time with his wife."

That wasn't a lie. Mr. Rudy's wife was in the early stages of dementia, so it was understandable that he wanted to spend time with his wife while she still had a decent grip on her memory. His request for a shorter route was the perfect opportunity for me to slide right in. Farad was right, the gods looked out big time.

I saw Els's head pop up when I said my name. Her hands adjusted her ponytail. My senses tuned in to her scent. *Almonds and vanilla.* That must have been her signature scent. I would find out soon enough when her hygiene items were in my bathroom and around our room.

Mr. Bill called out to Els, "Elsbeth, come over here and meet our new mail courier."

She said she was coming before she nervously walked over to where we stood. She fidgeted with the scrub top that she wore. Her face had no makeup. Her natural beauty was

37

all the makeup that she needed. "Hi, Thad. It's nice to see you again," she greeted.

"Oh, you two know each other?" Mr. Bill asked. He wore this cheesy smile when he asked. His eyes bounced between us.

My grin was inevitable. "Yes, sir, we do. It's nice to see you again as well. You look beautiful today. I can't wait until dinner Sunday with the fam."

I mentioned the dinner in front of Mr. Bill for a very particular reason. From what I heard he'd been married to his wife for over forty years. He took relationships seriously. In my opinion, I'd made it clear that I pined over Miss Elsbeth Draya Sanders. *I got her name from the ID in her wallet.* Now that I'd made it clear, I knew Mr. Bill was going to have my back and not let any of these crusty niggas roll up on her. It was important to have people working on your behalf when it came to this love thing.

"Oh, family dinner!" Mr. Bill's cheeks were high. "Mr. and Mrs. Sanders are amazing people." He wrapped his arm around Els. *I'on like that shit.* "It's nice to see a guy worth a damn liking you, baby girl."

Now Els's cheeks matched Mr. Bill's. "Mr. Bill, I don't mess with guys that are not worth a damn," she protested with her hand over her chest. She played like she was offended, but the smile on her face told me otherwise.

He chortled, then said, "If that's what you need to believe to sleep at night." After I handed him his mail, he said, "I'll leave you two to talk. Els, you can take a short break."

What the fuck did I say! I knew Mr. Bill was a man who would look out for a dapper, mature, young gentleman like me. He walked off to mind his drug business.

My hands clasped in front of me. "What's up, Beauty?" I decided that would be her nickname going forward.

"Why do you call me Beauty?" she reluctantly asked. I would think that would be obvious, but I didn't mind telling her.

I leaned toward her, put my lips near her ear, then said, "If no one has told you lately, you're simply beautiful. No additives are needed. From the day I saw you, I knew you were going to be my beauty."

My nose picked up a new scent. *Arousal.* I loved that shit because it was paramount to know that I could get her wet without touching her.

"Th-Thank you, Thad. That was very sweet." She shifted on her feet. It almost looked like she was about to start tap dancing.

I softly grabbed her hand. "It's the truth, Beauty. I'll see you later."

"I look forward to it." The flirtatiousness in her voice appealed to my dick. I knew her ass liked the man. I'm not a fucking kid.

The Next Day...

"Oh, please don't stop, Thad!" Enola was loud as hell. "Right there, right there!"

I was fucking the shit out of her like I normally did. Enola and I had been fucking on each other since we were in high school. Her father, Ahote, had been my father's spiritual advisor for almost as long as I'd been alive. With that being said, Enola and I spent a lot of time around each other. We dated for a short time in high school and a little after I came home from college.

In high school, we were too young to understand what it took to be in a relationship. After college, we were too old to tolerate each other. We were better as fuck partners no matter how much anyone in the pack thought we should be together.

"I'm about to nut, turn around and catch it." I groaned. When she pulled forward, I pulled the condom off and let loose in her mouth. My aim was shit so most of it got on her face, but she liked that shit. "That was a good fucking time, Enola."

She was a female that loved affirmations, so I tried to remember that. It made her happy and appreciative. When she was happy and appreciative, she fucked and sucked me better. It was a win-win.

She got up, walked in the bathroom that was connected to my bedroom, then turned on the sink faucet. I didn't need to see her to know that she was washing her face. A few minutes later, she came out of the bathroom with a clean face. "It was a good time. I need to get better at doing my Kegels, though, because the nigga I'm fucking with said I was feeling a little loose lately. Your big ass dick got him falling in," she said before she burst into laughter.

This seemed weird for her to talk about fucking other niggas in front of me, but that was the relationship that we had. She didn't want me any deeper than I wanted her. She was the perfect fuck buddy.

I joined her laughter. "You better get on that shit. I don't predict my dick getting any smaller. You could always find a nigga that matches my size. That's always an option," I joked.

She side-eyed me. "The only way that might happen

was if I fucked with a wolf. You know other than you, I'm good on wolf dick."

"Well, I don't know what to tell you, sweetheart," I commented with a titter. I put my back against the head-board of my bed. "You need to stop fucking around and just be with that nigga."

She paused her movement to look at me. "If only it could be that simple. You know just like I do that my father would not tolerate me being with a non-wolf for real." She snickered.

"Hell, you let them tell it, me and you are going to be together."

She was right. Our father had been advocating since we were in high school to be together and remain together. To them it just made sense for the Chief's son and Chief's spiritual advisor's daughter to come together as a unit. Everything that sounded good wasn't always good.

"Good thing we're not letting others tell our story for us," I said before grabbing my phone from the bedside table. "We let them dictate, we would have already had a strong litter of kids."

I noticed a notification from TikTok. When I opened it, my cheeks burned at the inbox from Elsbeth. Even her TikTok handle, @ElsBeauty4All, was beautiful. My finger couldn't tap the screen fast enough to open it. There was a reel attached. This had been how we communicated since I sent the first reel. In a day, we'd exchange multiple reels a day.

It was a reel from *TheRealKiloOfDope* ,who was a dope ass female trucker on TikTok. The sentiment of the reel basically was that we go together, and I better let these other bitches know. *I love this shit!* I shot her back the perfect response from this chick *Mahogany_musik* to show her my clock still had some crazy tick. Yeah, the exchange of these reels was full conversations between us. These two reels just exposed that we both had some crazy in us.

"Thad, do you hear me?" Enola's voice pulled my attention back to her. Nah, I didn't hear her. "What got you all caught up?"

I flung the covers off my lap, then swung my legs around. "My business got me caught up. I'll see you another time. Make sure you lock the door on your way out."

Enola's ass was nosy as hell. It wasn't just my business; it was anyone's business that didn't belong to her. "Well dang, Thaddeus. I wasn't trying to get in all your business." She giggled softly. "You coming by tomorrow?"

"Nah, I'm going to be in Raleigh next week," I said as I walked toward my bathroom. "I'll be here for the campfire stories."

She sucked her teeth. "You know, Thad, I'm not sure if you know, but there is a post office here in Lumberton as well. I don't know why you rather work in Raleigh that's damn near two hours away." She crossed her arms over her chest. "You have a big ass house here that is paid for, but you are paying mortgage on a condo that's in Raleigh. That's ass backwards to me," she concluded.

There she was in business that wasn't her own. She assumed there was a mortgage on my condo, but I bought it with cash. Again, my family was far from broke. Our casino brought in extremely good money along with other businesses that were family owned. On top of that, when I was not at my apartment, I listed it on Airbnb. Farad's condo was on the floor below. Both of our condos had two bedrooms.

We would alternate months when it came to the listing of our condos. One month, he listed his place and if he

42

stayed in Raleigh he stayed at my place. It was the same when I listed my place. In a month, we could pull in eight to twelve thousand dollars a month. It was a good side hustle that we had without thinking about it.

"Yes, Lumberton does have a post office. The post office here has nothing to do with the post office that I chose to work at in Raleigh where I want to work." I turned to give her a final look. "Make sure you lock up. I got shit to do and I need to wash my dick."

"You are such an asshole sometimes," she said with a snarky smile. This was another reason we couldn't be together. We secretly got on each other's nerves.

I didn't give her the satisfaction of a response. My body stepped fully into the bathroom, then the door closed after me. On Saturdays, I made sure to get mail out early so I could get my ass back to Lumberton to spend time with my parents for dinner.

About two hours later, I was walking into my parents' house which was next door to mine. My parent's house sat in the middle with my house and my sister's house flanking theirs. I loved both my parents; however, my mom was easier to love than my dad.

"Hey, Ma, you look beautiful today like always." I kissed her cheek where she stood at the stove stirring a pot. My mother's youthful appearance had my father going crazy on niggas on a regular when they were out.

She turned the eye of the stove down before she turned to face me. "Let me look at my grown baby boy." She poked and prodded at me. "You look fine to me," she said before she put her finger on her chin. "That gives me so much pause."

I didn't want to fall in the trap, but I knew that it would save so much time to just fall. See, Parie Lourie will hold you hostage until you fall. If you choose not to fall, then she will push your ass. "Why does that give you pause, Ma?"

She grabbed her thermal of water, moved to the kitchen island, then took a seat. "When I decided to go into the medical field, I was excited about knowing one day that I would be the person to be the doctor to bring my grandchildren into the world. I've assisted with many litters being born in this tribe, but here are my daughter and son in their thirties with no children. Y'all just don't want me to be happy. All my friends bragging on their lopsided head grandbabies, and I have none to brag about."

It was important that there were doctors and midwives in every pack. When a wolf had a baby, you could never be sure what the outcome would be. The offspring of wolves often came out with alluring eyes that couldn't be ignored. Also, the women were not always pregnant for nine months.

"Ma, do you just want me to go out and put random babies in these women just to satisfy your need to have grandbabies? That doesn't sound very logical." She was tripping at this point.

My mother didn't take her eyes off me as she drank her water through the straw of her tumbler. Once she'd gotten all the hydration she wanted, she put the cup down. "Thaddeus, I would have thought you and Enola would have a baby by now." Her hand flew up. "I know y'all have no interest with being in a relationship, but as much as you two have sex, I would think that y'all would slip up by now." She tittered, then said, "I just knew y'all was going to be teenage parents."

"Dang, Ma! Tell me how you really feel." I was a little surprised by her admission. It was the first time she had ever said some shit like that. "I'm surprised you'd ever want me to have a baby with Enola considering you don't really like the girl."

Her shoulders lifted, then dropped. "My not liking her clearly has nothing to do with your penis liking her vagina." Her curtsy smile was amusing. "Like I said, I would have thought there would be a slip by now."

There was no way that I would ever tell her that we did have a slip in our early twenties. We were both in college but were still fucking around since our colleges were close. When she found out that she was pregnant, she wasn't one hundred percent sure who the father was. She was dealing with two other dudes outside of me but fucked me the most. She decided the best decision was to terminate the pregnancy. I had no issue with that, and afterward, I made sure I stayed strapped up.

"Well, I'm sorry to disappoint you, Ma." I shook my head and laughed. "When Els, I mean the right girl—"

My mother's head snapped in my direction where I stood near the refrigerator. "No, you won't ski over your little slip like I didn't hear you." Her cheeks brightened. "Who is Els?"

I wanted to kick my own ass. Let me rip the band aid off. I wanted to have this conversation once so I could set boundaries early. "Els or Elsbeth, is the female that's going to be my mate."

My mother choked up a little before she was on her feet. "Your mate! Elsbeth," she said more to herself. "Wait, isn't that the girl from the party at the hotel? I didn't realize she was a wolf."

I knew that was coming. *Here goes nothing.* "She's not a wolf."

My mother gazed at me for a moment. I knew that was something that she expected to hear. This was actually the first time that I'd told her about a girl that I was interested in. I knew she was going to be completely vested. I knew how my father felt about wolves mating with humans, but I had never broached the subject with my mother.

A soft smile arose on her face. She walked over to me, placed a hand on each cheek, then tilted my head down. Our eyes locked. "I only want to know does she make your heart smile?"

I didn't have to take any time to think about my answer. "Ma, I haven't been in her presence more than four times. Every time I am, I know that I would rearrange the solar system to move the Earth between Jupiter and Saturn in the solar system if she told me the sun was too hot." My chest swelled. "I'm having dinner at her parents' house tomorrow with Farad and Rummie."

"Well, if you feel that way, then yes, she will be your mate. Now, what we're going to do is keep this to ourselves for a little while." Her smile dropped slightly. "Your father won't be happy, but what he wants doesn't trump your heart's desire."

My mother's approval wasn't needed because I would do what my heart pulled me to do anyway. The fact that she gave me her approval meant everything. I knew my father's approval wouldn't come easily, if it came at all.

Elsbeth

Guess Who's Coming to Dinner...

"Sis, you look amazing. Stop fidgeting with your hair," Mi fussed. For the past hour, she had been fussing at me.

We were in my bedroom at my parents' house. Thad, Farad, and Rummie would be here soon. I'd changed my outfits three times and would have changed it again if Mi didn't threaten to fight me. My hair changed just as many times as my outfits. It was up, then it was down. It was half up, half down and braided in a fish braid. I started to change my hair again, but I knew Mi would commit violence after she was the one who braided my hair.

"Fine and thank you." I stood in front of the mirror. Yes, she was correct. I looked amazing. I was just nervous to be in Thad's presence.

Since the first day that he came into the pharmacy to deliver the mail, I'd seen him almost every day. He not only did the mail delivery to my job, but he also did the delivery to my apartment complex. At first, I thought it was weird before Mi pointed out that our complex wasn't far from our job. It made sense that both places would be on the same route. That man looked good in anything that he had on.

When he was at the mail unit in my apartment complex, I knew that I couldn't get my mail because it was against the law since he was putting the mail in. That didn't matter because I still found myself parking near it and watching him. I acted like I was reading, but I knew that he knew better. The first day, he walked over after he finished with my mail and hand delivered it to me.

Now, I wanted him to hand deliver something else to my body flower. I decided to wear a cute, clingy, but not too tight bodysuit. I wanted to wear a pair of Crocs, but my mother and Mi said they would beat me up. The women in my life were so violent. Now I was wearing a pair of skateboard causal shoes that I almost had to beg to wear. They wanted me to wear heels, and I told them they lost their minds. I was never going to do anything just to impress anyone.

There was a knock on the door before my father came into the room. He stopped at the door and just stared at me. With a cheeky smile, he said, "You didn't tell me that you liked this fella." My eyes bucked at him. *How in the hell does he know that I like him?* "I know when my daughter puts a little extra something on her appearance. You rarely wear mascara, baby girl."

"See, I told you that you were doing too much with the mascara and eyeliner crap." Mi insisted that I put on a little makeup. I didn't want to but here I was with damn eyeliner, mascara, and my brows done.

Mi beamed with pride. "Doesn't she look amazing, Pop

Harry? All I wanted to do was accentuate her natural beauty."

My father strolled over to me with his head high, shoulders back, and chest out. He was such a handsome man. My parents had been together since they were teenagers, broke up during college, but were back together before they graduated. They were my prototype for what I wanted my relationships and marriage to be.

"Baby girl, Mi didn't do too much. You are gorgeous with or without makeup. I'm sure that nigga knows too," he said before he kissed my cheek. The corner of his rose. "The way that nigga is down there fidgeting with his best clothes on tells me that he likes you too."

Now that I knew that Thad was downstairs, I was more nervous. "They're downstairs?"

"That's why I'm up here now. Let me escort my beautiful baby girl downstairs," my daddy said before he offered me his arm.

I took it with excitement and pride. After I accepted, he offered Mi his other arm which she accepted. Like two princesses on the arms of a King, my father escorted us downstairs. When we walked into the dining room, I noticed my mother had already set the food on the table. She went all out too.

"Wow, Mama, you made my favorite." My eyes quickly traveled to Thad. When our eyes connected, I focused back on the food. "I love lambchops."

My mother crossed her arms over her chest. "Now, I know I raised a more respectful daughter than one that walks into a room that doesn't speak to everyone in the room." *There she goes, embarrassing me.*

"Mama, I was going to speak," I said with a nervous

laugh. "You know I love lambchops." I walked over to Rummie first. "Hey, Rummie, thanks for coming."

She opened her arms, then pulled me into a hug. "I wouldn't want to be anywhere else." She pulled back, looked at me, then said, "You look so beautiful."

Even if I didn't want to blush, my cheeks had other plans. "Thank you, Rummie." I moved to Farad next, who also stood and gave me a hug. When I got to Thad, my nerves got the best of me. I stuck my hand out. "Thank you for coming, Thad."

He looked down at my hand with a scrunched face. "How does everyone else get a hug, but you're sticking your hand out to me?" I couldn't tell if he was joking or not.

I glanced over at my daddy. His brow arched, then he said, "You better give that man a hug. The hell you looking at me for?"

Slowly, my head turned back to Thad. He stood there with nose turned up. "Can I have my hug now, Miss Elsbeth?"

I walked into his opened arms. When he wrapped them around me, it felt like my knees buckled a little bit. My body melted into his. He smelled like all of my hopes, dreams, and ambitions. His lips kissed my temple, and my body flower lost her damn mind. I had never pulled away from someone so fast. "Let's eat."

I moved around the table to sit down only to realize that there wasn't a seat for me on that side. There was only one seat that was not occupied when I looked around the table. It couldn't be right though. "Mama, where do I sit?"

"Girl, I know you see that seat right there," my mother quipped. "Go sit down."

Mikayla had the giggles tonight I see. Everything was overly funny to her for some reason. I slowly made my way over to the seat that was between Rummie and Thad. With all of this showing out that my parents were doing, I could only assume that they liked Thaddeus. *I wonder how long they were down here before my father came up.*

After we said grace, serving dishes were passed around. "Mrs. Sanders, all of this looks amazing," Rummie complimented. "We're going to invite you all over to our parents' house for dinner. You haven't had lamb until you've had it unprocessed."

Dinner at his parents' house! I wasn't going to say anything about that. My head tilted. "Unprocessed, what does that mean?"

"Oh." Thad spoke up. "We're from Lumberton, North Carolina and we live on the Lumbee reservation. There is a farm on the reservation as well as gardens. All of our food comes from the land." There was so much pride in his voice. "We have our own butcher house on the reservation as well."

"Oh, wow! I would have never thought that any of you were Native Americans," Mi said with an elevated pitch. "Oh, I'm so sorry. That sounded racist."

Rummie chuckled before she waved her hand. "Girl, you're fine. People are always thrown off when they see what they call black Indians. We're used to it."

"Oh, there's nothing better than some country food cooking," my daddy said. "Do y'all have deer meat? I know I can't buy any, but I'm willing to barter for some."

Farad burst into laughter. "Not the retired sheriff talking about he wants to barter." He snickered for a little while longer, then waved my daddy off. "Nah, you can come through and get some meat."

"You don't have to tell me but once," my daddy said with a bright smile. "I haven't had deer in years. I used to

51

have a friend that hunted, but he moved across the country."

We had a boisterous conversation about a bunch of different things. As the evening went on, I became more and more relaxed. Mi told a funny joke that caused me to laugh so hard that Thad put his hand on my thigh because it sounded like I would stop breathing. When his hand gripped my thigh, I wanted to lay his ass on the table and take him down.

My mother made a red velvet and a chocolate, almond layer cake. After we all had cake on our plate, we started to eat. My father stopped eating his cake after a few bites, then put his spoon down. He cleared his throat, gathering the attention of the table.

"Thad and Farad, not only from man to man, also from me as a father, I wanted to thank you both." His voice cracked a little, but he got himself together. "You two protected my daughter when I couldn't. There is nothing that I could ever think to do to ever repay you."

I didn't think that I had ever seen my father get emotional, especially in front of me. My heart broke. "Daddy, I'm sorry. If I would have never gone to the party like Mikayla told me to..."

I just wanted my daddy to not hurt. I should have stayed my black ass home and none of it would have happened. Shakina barely spoke to me at school until a few weeks ago. I thought it was weird, but I brushed it off when I shouldn't have. I should have trusted my instincts.

Mikayla jumped up from her seat. "I know good and well you're not blaming yourself for what those sick fucks tried to do to you." She turned to my mother. "Forgive me for my language."

"Please proceed as you were," my mother said. She

waved her off, sat back, then crossed her arms over her chest. Her deep stare never left me.

My best friend turned her attention back to me. "None of this is your fault. Those fuckas are sick. You should be able to go anywhere you want and not have to worry about someone potentially raping you."

I knew she was right, but I just hated hearing the hurt in my daddy's voice. The pad of Thad's finger under my eye shocked me. I didn't know that I was crying. Also, every time he touched me, electricity shot through my body. When I peeked over to him, his expression was soft.

"Beauty, you did nothing wrong," he said in a feathery voice. "No one will ever hurt you." He paused to give my father a warm smile. "As long as you have me, anyone linked to me, and your people, I promise on everything that makes me who I am that you will be safe."

The conviction in his voice told me that he meant every letter and syllable of every word that he said. What was more amazing was that I believed him with everything in me. "Thank you, Thad. It makes me feel good knowing I have someone like you on my side."

His lips landed on my temple again. After a short silence, my father finished his apology. Once desert was over, it was still early and just in time for football. Of course, my daddy invited them into his coveted man cave that me nor my mother were allowed in. Before they went into the cave, Thad asked if he could have a word with me. I took him to the backyard for privacy.

"I just wanted to thank you again for inviting us to dinner with your family. It was good as hell," he complimented. "Can you cook like you mom?" His smile was so gorgeous.

With a smile that matched his, I said, "I surely can.

She's had me in the kitchen with her since I was five or six. I was going to learn how to cook by any means necessary."

"Cool, good to know for our future." He took a step closer to me. "So, I wanna take you out on a date."

I heard his words, but I was still stuck on him mentioning our future. Ours, as in together. I snapped back into the conversation. "Oh, I don't know if that's a good idea, Thad."

He stared at me for a moment. "Okay, I'm not going to beg you. I'll give you a week and come back to give you the details." He leaned into me, pecked my lips, then walked off.

What the hell just happened? In my mind, I replayed, telling him that I didn't think it was a good idea. I needed to make sure that's what happened. Based on what Thad said before he walked off, I was going on a date with him at some point regardless of me not thinking it was a good idea. I didn't want to think about the peck he gave me with his pillow soft lips. Although I didn't want to think about it, my body flower had already imagined them kissing her.

I shook off the interaction before I went into the den with the other women. Their conversation stopped the second I stepped into the room. I stopped, looked around, then asked, "What's wrong?"

"It ain't no, what's wrong," Mi blurted. "You better sit down and tell us what that was about."

My mother wasn't any better than my best friend. Rummie came in at a quick third. I rolled my eyes before I plopped down on the couch. "That was about nothing. He just asked me out on a date."

My mother sat forward. "When are y'all going out? Make sure you tell him to pick you up from here. I want to do your hair." She pointed at Mikayla. "You can style her." She pointed at me next. "You will wear heels too, lil girl."

They planned a date that I declined. Rummie had even joined in on the planning with enthusiasm. It didn't escape me when she said that her brother had never been interested in any female like he was with me. That brought a smile to my face. I let them plan for a few more minutes before I interrupted. "First, I declined the offer."

"Lil girl, say what?" Her high grating tone was not a surprise. Marci Sanders thought she ran my life sometimes, especially when it came to my dating life. "Give me one good reason that you can't go out with Thaddeus, Elsbeth Darya Sanders."

Not my whole government name. "Mama, just because he saved me doesn't mean that I'm obligated to date him. I thanked him appropriately and so did you and Daddy."

My mother relaxed in her seat before she crossed one leg over the other. "I didn't ask you if you were obligated to do anything. What I asked you was to give me one good reason you couldn't go out with him. It's clear that you're not obligated to do a damn thing."

I didn't have a reason outside of the one I thought was good enough. "Mama, I mean based on what he said when I told him that I didn't think it was a good idea, it sounds like we're going out anyway."

When Mi asked what he said, Rummie jumped in. "I'll tell you what he said. He ignored her scary ass and told her he was still going to be taking her out at some point." She leaned forward, looked at my mother and asked her to beg her pardon with what she was about to say. "Els, every time you look at my brother your eyes fuck him."

A gasp left my mouth, and my eyeballs almost fell out of their sockets. My mother doubled over in laughter. I was shocked into silence. "Rummie, I thought I was the only one that noticed that," my mother added. "I just didn't want to say anything in front of her daddy."

"Whatever, I was not." I rebutted. "I was looking at him like I was looking at everyone. He's not special," I lied.

I didn't understand why I was making this so hard. I really didn't have a reason not to go out with Thad, but I was scared. It wasn't like I was quote-unquote inexperienced with men. I haven't been in an official relationship since college, but I had no issue when I wanted to get some peen. I could admit that sometimes I missed certain signs of attraction from men, but that was more their fault than mine. The dudes these days were weird with how they showed their interest in women.

My mother stood from her seat. "I'm going to get a bottle of wine and some glasses. While I do that, Elsbeth, you carry your ass down to that basement and tell Thad that you changed your mind."

She walked out of the den. I didn't have a chance to pushback which sucked. My pout presented itself boldly. *I'm not doing shit.* When my mother came back into the den with the wine and glasses, she stopped at the doorway.

With a tight face, she said, "Oh, okay. I see you want me to tell him." She put the bottle and glasses down on the side table. "I don't have a problem with that."

I jumped up. "Okay, Mama!" I popped my hip out. "How is my mother making me go on a date? This feels so abrasive."

Mi kissed her teeth. "Els, stop being so freaking dramatic. You know good and well that you want to go out with that man. Stop postponing the inevitable, best friend."

Like a child, I pouted and stomped out of the den toward the basement staircase. The door was closed as expected, so I rang the video doorbell. Yes, my father's extra ass had a doorbell.

"Yeah, baby girl." His voice came through the speaker.

"Daddy, sorry to bother y'all. Can you send Thaddeus up here? I need to talk to him for a second," I asked.

He let me know that he would send him up. I took a step back, because I would look crazy if I was standing directly in front of the door when he opened it. A minute later, the door opened. Thad stepped into the hallway, then closed the door behind him. My father must have given him the door code to get back into the basement. When my father said that we weren't allowed in his man cave without his permission, he meant that. My mother had the door code and I'm sure he knew, but he had never said anything to my knowledge.

"What's up, Beauty?" His voice was hard to get over because the deep-set drawl of it would make anyone's pussy wet. That, combined with his overly attractive, chocolate skin, beard, and just amazingness was a dangerous combination.

"Um, I wanted to let you know that I changed my mind about the date thing," I rambled out. "You can let me know when. I'll let you know if my schedule is clear."

He lowered his shaking head. I heard his light chuckles but was unsure of what was funny. When he lifted his head, his stare was void of any humor. "Elsbeth, Beauty, let's get this out of the way. I sent you the date information shortly after our little conversation." He paused to give time for the confusion to showcase. "I'm not about to play this back-and-forth shit with you.

"I like you. I want you, and I feel the feeling is mutual." He crossed his arms over himself. "Tell me I'm wrong and

I'll pull the date back. Once I pull the date back, there will not be another request."

I wanted to lie and tell him that the feeling wasn't mutual. Something told me that if I did that, I would regret it. I did like him, and he seemed like a great guy. My parents clearly liked his ass, so that test was passed. "I mean, yes, I do like you."

"Okay, so let's both be adults here," he retorted. "I'm not going to do all this extra shit with you when you're my woman. Trust me, you wouldn't want me to either. Raleigh's population doesn't need that kind of rapid decrease." He invaded my face. "Now, there's no need to tell me whether you're free or not. I know you're not working, and you don't have class."

How the hell? "How do you know that I don't have to work?" He must have talked to Mikayla.

He put his lips next to my ear. "I'm always going to know everything I need to know about you. You'll soon have the same privileges and so many more."

The warmth from his breath tickled my ear before the kiss tickled it even more. Without a goodbye, he spun on his feet, put the code in the door, opened it, then walked in being sure to close it behind him. Once again, my mind only had one question: *What the hell just happened?*

Date Night...

Thad didn't tell a lie. When I got back to the den the night of our Sunday dinner, there was a text on my phone with the date of our date and the time to be ready. When I saw that he said he would pick me up from my parents' house, it was at that moment that I knew my parents had something to do with this whole date initiative. The women were still planning my date.

Well, here we are a weekend later and it was date night. Tonight was a replica of Sunday because I changed outfits three times. The biggest difference tonight was I was not the reason for the wardrobe changes. The third outfit was a pair of skinny jeans, with a fitted t-shirt that said *God's Favor*. On my feet were a pair of heels that I desperately wanted to take off. I walked in heels like a pro thanks to the many lessons from my mother when I was younger. The fact that I could walk in them like a pro didn't negate the fact that I hated wearing them.

My mother was doing the final touches on my hair while Mikayla was making sure the makeup that she applied was perfect. She didn't do a lot, but it was more than I was used to. After a twenty-minute argument, I allowed her to put lashes on me. I hated how great I looked with these damn lashes on.

"You look so beautiful," my mama said after she placed the final hair accessory in the bun that she'd placed in my hair. "He's gonna be all over you."

"Mama, I don't need to dress like this to have him all over me," I snapped back. I hated it when people equated beauty with makeup and heels. I was never a girl who liked wearing heels and makeup because I was a tomboy. My mama got a rude awakening when she thought she was going to have this little princess, but instead my daddy got a road dog.

My mama leaned down, kissed my cheek, then said, "I know, baby. I know."

My dad yelled for us to come downstairs. My mama and Mi said they would go down first, then I had to wait a minute then come down. You would have thought I was coming down to meet my prom date. Once my Mama and Mikayla left, I counted to sixty before I came to the top of the stairs. Daddy, Mama, Mi, and Thad were standing at the bottom with their heads lifted and sight on me. Thad's smile made me smile.

I started my trek down the stairs. I was nervous as hell. My prayer that I didn't bust my ass down these stairs was a real thing.

Thad walked up and met me halfway. His lips pressed lightly against mine. He glanced down at my feet. "You wanted to wear those?"

I kissed my teeth. Since dinner we had been texting and talking on the phone. We still did our reel flirting on TikTok as I called it. I loved talking to him on the phone. "You know good and well these shoes were not my choice."

He stepped up to be on the same step as me. "Take your ass in that room and put on the shoes you want to wear. We talked about this."

It was ironic that he said we talked about me doing what I wanted to do. "You fussing about me doing what others told me to do, but I'm about to go on a date that you told me I was going on. How does that work?"

"We're going on a date that you wanted to go on." Thad's cockiness was on front street. "You came to your daddy's man cave to get me. You told me that you changed your mind, so we're on date that you wanted to go on." He pecked my lips again. "Besides, heels won't be comfortable at the drag racetrack."

The raunchy side of me thought it was sexy that he didn't give a damn that he was in front of my parents and still kissed me. I glanced around him to my mama and best friend. "He said I could change my shoes." I stuck my tongue out at them before I took off back up the stairs.

It wasn't until I got to my room and slipped on my skater sneakers that I realized he said we were going to the drag racetrack. My excitement piqued. Thad and I had conversations about how much I loved drag racing but had never been to one personally. Without thinking, I rushed out of my room. I ran down the stairs before Thad could make it up halfway to meet me. "Did you say we're going to the track?"

Everyone chuckled. "Yes, Beauty, that's what I said. Are you ready to go?"

Just like that, we were out of the door. It was cool that he drove a Jeep and really had ducks in the windshield. I would have never pegged him for a man that would keep the ducks when he was ducked. From our talks I knew this wasn't his only vehicle, but the one he used when he was in Raleigh. On the way to the track, we talked about his collection of ducks. I wanted a Jeep just to be ducked, but my parents said that wasn't enough of a reason to gain a car note.

"This is amazing." I beamed with admiration as we stood on the side of the track enjoying the activities. There were so many people at the track. "I would love to come to these more often."

The crowd was so diverse. I especially loved seeing the female racers. Thad told me that he loved drag racing too, that's what sparked the conversation. His love was clear because when we got here a lot of people knew him. He made sure to always introduce me as his woman. I wasn't sure when that was established, but we'd talk about that later.

Thad wrapped his arms around me from behind. "We

can come whenever you want, Beauty." He kissed my neck. "You want anything else to eat?"

Oh, that was another thing. I loved, loved, loved food trucks. When we got here and I saw there were food trucks, I counted them. Twenty food trucks—there were twenty food trucks out here of all types. Thad told me there were about six hundred people out here if not more. "No, I think your woman has had enough." The sarcasm was real when I peeked over my shoulder up at him.

His cheeks lifted before he burst into laughter. As he laughed, I turned in his arms with the corner of my lip crooked. "What? You have a problem being my woman?"

"I'm just trying to figure out when we had that conversation. Perhaps, if I remembered the conversation, then I would remember me agreeing to be your woman." My arms were wrapped around his waist.

He looked down at me, kissed my lips deeply, then said, "Let me tell you when we had a conversation about you being my woman. When you sent me that reel on TikTok and I sent you one back. We've been sending reels to each other for a while now. You send me reels, I send you reels, so that mean that we're in a real relationship." He took a step back, but kept his arms wrapped around me. "Beauty, if I find out you're out here sending reels to other niggas, we're going to have a real problem."

Is he serious? When he didn't break a smile, I had my answer. There was no need to act like I didn't want to be his girl, but I just couldn't fold like freshly dried laundry on the first damn date. "So, you know you want me to be your woman on the first date?"

"Nah, I knew I wanted you to be my woman the second you walked into that ballroom at the hotel," he confirmed. "See, that's why I paid close attention to everything that was going on around you. Before you were mine, you were mine to protect, and I took that shit serious from millisecond one." He tapped my lips with his. "Stop making this shit difficult so we came move this relationship forward."

Right there in his arms, I conceded. "Well, I guess you have a woman, and I have a man. That escalated quickly."

Thaddeus

A Little Time Later...

Tonight was our bi-monthly campfire gathering on the reservation. It was a chance for members of our tribe and pack to come together and spend time with each other. Sometimes people assumed that if you were a member of the tribe that you were also a member of the pack. That wasn't true because not everyone in the tribe was a wolf. I won't lie and say that there wasn't elitism within the tribe. The ones that were wolves felt the gods bestowed a gift on them because they were set apart.

"You going to Raleigh after the pack meeting?" Farad asked from his seat next to me. "Your ass been missing since you got a meeting. Even Enola said something about the shit the other day."

Normally, I was in Raleigh, but today was different. Our pack meetings could last well into the night, and if we decide to hunt, then it could be the early morning. "Nah, Els and Mikayla are on their way here now. Els is staying with me tonight. As far as Enola, she'll be all right."

Since Elsbeth openly acknowledged that I was her man and she was my woman, naturally, I cut off all sexual relationships with anyone that I was dealing with. It wasn't like I had a haram, but I had a few in rotation. Enola was the only female that I didn't block because she was a member of the pack, plus it was nothing like that. She had a nigga she was fucking with and wanted to be with. Her daddy was her issue with that since he wasn't a wolf. She's asked to fuck, and I've told her I was good.

"Wait, Els is coming here?" He looked around. "Like here with the pack and tribe? With your daddy sitting over there with the elders?" I heard the disbelief in his voice, and it was understandable. "Damn, you making your debut like that, my boy?"

He was right. The pack would immediately know that she didn't have a beast the second she was near. Wolves always sensed other wolves. That would bring a lot of pause and questions that I was ready for. I didn't mind answering questions as long as no one disrespected my woman. "My dad will be all right as well. He can control a lot of things, but not my personal life. Elsbeth Darya Sanders will be my mate sooner than even she thinks."

As if I wrote the scene myself, my senses opened to the scent of my woman. That's one of the main indicators that I knew she was my mate. Out of all the females that I'd ever dealt with, including Enola, my beast had never acknowledged their scent. My beast got excited when she was in our presence. "They're here."

Farad stood with me and fell in step when I moved toward the scent. The nervousness was all over my baby's face. The closer we got to each other, the more my wolf anxiety rose right along with my dick. "Hey, Beauty."

She walked into my opened arms with a wide smile.

"Hey, baby." She stood on her tip toes to meet me halfway with her lips. She looked around at everyone around our gathering spot. "There's a lot of people out here."

"You're safe with me. You know that." I patted her ass. "What's up, Mikayla?"

She didn't respond because she was too busy scoping the scene. We stood there giving her ass time to take it in. After another minute, she finally responded. "Okay, Farad and Thad, I'm going to point them out and you tell me whether they are worth introducing me to them. Now don't lie because y'all know I'm bat shit crazy. I will kill a nigga, cook dinner, call the cops, and tell them I have a plate and a dead body waiting for them."

Farad threw his head back in laughter. "Bruh, you're crazy as fuck. I know a couple of these boys that love that crazy shit." He grabbed her hand. "Come on, I got you, sis."

Mi snatched her hand from him. "Boy, stop before they think we're together. I'on want no one to mistake you for my man."

She was serious as hell and that pulled the laughter out of me. Sis wasn't playing about getting her man. The pack was already in my head asking who she was. They weren't going to ask me about Els, because her in my arms told them all they needed to know. *"Y'all calm down. Farad is about to bring her over there to meet y'all. Aye, I'm going to say this once, Mikayla is my woman's sister which means that she's my family."*

That was all I needed to say. They knew what my words implied. From my words alone, I knew that a few of them would fall back because they played nothing but games. They wouldn't risk going against me, and at this point Farad, for hurting Mikayla because of their inability to be a man. I gave Beauty another kiss, then told her it was time to meet my tribe.

I got halfway through introducing her to people when Enola took it upon herself to approach us. Her eyes had been on us the entire time that I was walking Beauty around introducing her. Before Beauty got here, I knew that I would introduce her to my parents last since I figured they'd want to sit down and talk to us.

"Hey, Thaddeus, who do we have here?" Enola wore a smile, but something told me that she wasn't happy. *She better not be on some bullshit because it's going to be a situation.*

"What's up, Enola? This is my woman, Elsbeth. Elsbeth, this is Enola. Her father is my father's spiritual advisor." I introduced her like I always did, but now her attitude told me she expected more.

Beauty smiled. "Hey, Enola, it's so nice to meet you." She looked at me with a snarky smile. "How long have you and Thad known each other?" After Enola confirmed that we've known each other all our lives, she said, "Ow, I bet you got some good stories."

Enola looked between the two of us. "Do I! We're definitely going to have to get together sometimes."

Maggie, Jorie, and Rummie came up to us just in the nick of time. "Hey, Elsbeth! When Rummie told us you were coming, I was so excited," Jorie said.

Her, Mikayla, and Els had been hanging out at school from what I was told. I liked that shit for multiple reasons. I wanted her to be protected at all times. I knew it was logical that I couldn't be everywhere at all times, so someone in my pack being around her made me feel better.

"I'm so happy that my baby invited me and Mi," Els

responded. She looked around, then snickered. "Mi is over there being fresh."

All of our attention turned in the direction of where she was looking. Mi sat at the fire with Sabastian looking real cozy. He was a good guy, so I didn't have to problem with that. Sabastian was a thirty-year-old single father. His son's mother dipped on him when their child was eight months old. That girl sent Sebastian a message to come to her house. He walked in and his son was in his car seat on the kitchen counter with a note saying she had better things to do with her time than be a mother.

Being a single parent can mature any person quick as hell. His son, Sabian, was four now. "Oh, it looks like you brought another one here to steal from the pack."

Enola's voice snapped all of us out of our surveillance of Mikayla. Her brash mention of the pack had me on high alert. Was she out of her fucking mind?

Beauty's hand tightened around mine before her head tilted. "I'm sorry, I'm not sure what that means? Would you mind giving me clarity, Enola, is it?" She released my hand and crossed her arms over herself. "I'm not sure if I missed something. Is that your man?" she asked after she pointed at Mikayla and Sabastian.

Oh, my baby is with the shenanigans. Enola actually looked shocked, like she didn't expect Els to say anything. When I noticed Enola's fangs slightly protrude, I jumped into action. "She doesn't mean shit by it. Enola, let me holla at you real quick."

There was no chance for her to accept or decline the invitation before my hand was around her arm to pull her off to the side. Once we were out of earshot from anyone, I let my fangs show. The growl left my pit before I had a chance to stop it. "Have you lost your fucking mind? How dare you disrespect my mate?"

In a low register, she responded, "Your mate?" She moved into my personal space. "Your fucking mate? Are you serious right now? You're asking me how I disrespected your mate when you're comfortable with disrespecting me."

Now I was lost as fuck. I took a large step back because no woman would be in my space like that if her name wasn't Elsbeth Darya Sanders. "Please tell me how the hell I'm disrespecting you by bringing my woman to meet my people. You're on some real good bullshit with your attitude and mentioning the pack in mixed company."

She let out a loud *ha.* "Mixed company, you say. You're out here introducing her as your mate, but you just said that she's mixed fucking company. Does she know you're from a pack of wolves, Thaddeus?"

Yep, I introduced her to my people as my mate. They needed to know my intention and I wasn't ashamed to make that clear. "What she knows is none of your concern. If I remember correctly, you're not my woman, never have been my woman, will never be my woman, and most importantly, you don't want to be my damn woman. You got a whole nigga that you're scared to tell your daddy about. Don't bring that shit this way because I don't give a fuck."

The nail was hit on the head, and she knew it. Her face was tight as hell and my beast was responding to the feistiness of her beast, and not in a good way. As far as my beast was concerned, Els was our mate.

Enola cut her eyes. "You can talk all the big dog shit you want," she disrespectfully said. That big dog shit she said could get her slaughtered. "From the way your father is over there scowling tells me that little relationship you think you're in won't go too far." She walked to my side. "Have fun with that shit."

By the time I got back over to the girls, Mikayla joined them. Based on the arched brow, tight lips, and hand on her hip, I knew she was debriefed on Enola's little show. I refused to address the shit.

I wrapped my arms around Beauty, kissed her lips, then said, "Let me introduce you to my parents. They're right over here." I pointed toward my parents' direction.

"I hope they're nicer than your ex-girlfriend." Her stare was hard as fuck. "Make sure you tell her that I fight bitches. Don't my small stature fool you." With a warm smile, she said, "Let's go meet your parents."

I smiled at her resilience because although she had an attitude, I knew it wasn't with me. Our hands clasped, then I led her to my parents who were sitting among the elders. My mother sat there fidgeting with excitement. The entire time I introduced Beauty to others, she was in my ear asking when I was going to bring her to them.

"Ma, Dad, I want to introduce you to my mate, Elsbeth. Elsbeth, these are my parents, Patrick and Parie Lourie." I didn't want my father to know that Els had already met my ma.

My mother popped up, pulled Els into a hug, then said, "Hey, baby! It's so nice to see you again." She pulled back from the hug. "Girl, you look good!"

"I look good! No, you look good," Els complimented. She looked over my mother's shoulder at my father. "Hi, Mr. Lourie, how are you tonight?"

When she extended her hand to shake, he shook it, but his eyes remained on me. *"Your mate, Thaddeus? This is who you are choosing to claim as your mate?"* He mind spoke to me instead of responding to Els. When I didn't answer, he finally responded to her. "It's nice to meet you, young lady. Sit down, so we can talk."

My parents separated to allow us to sit between them. The other elders introduced themselves, then gave us some privacy. My father asked about her and her family as soon as she sat down. He was impressed with her father being a retired sheriff and her mother being a retired teacher. He was even more impressed with her being in school to become a pharmacist. That was my mother's chance to add her two cents. "Oh, that's amazing. We're working on opening a general store and we wanted to include a pharmacy!"

That was true and I'd thought about that myself. We'd have time to have that conversation after we mate and she moved in with me. I sat there listening to my father interview her. He was attentive and hadn't tried to mind speak with me the entire time he spoke to her. *This may fare out better than I thought it would.*

"Elsbeth, has my son told you the lineage of the Lumbee Tribe?" my father asked with his eyes slightly tightened and head leaned to the side. He glanced at me for a second before he focused back on Els.

She must have felt the sudden tension in his tone. Els shifted in her seat uncomfortably. "Um, no he hasn't. When he told me that he was a part of the tribe, I did some research. I learned a lot of interesting history and cultural information."

I grabbed her hand in admiration. She never told me that she did research on my people. He asked her what she learned, and she was excited to tell him.

"Son, you call her your mate, but haven't told her about your beast? That's shameful." My father reprimanded me. That was to be expected.

I shrugged. *"She will know when it is important for her to know. It will be in our time, not yours."*

That answer didn't make him happy. My mother had been a silent observer for most of the conversation. *"Patrick, leave him alone. Elsbeth is wonderful for our son. Now stop all this mind speak while she's telling us what she learned."* Her words didn't please him any more than mine did.

"I commend you for doing your research. There is a lot of good history available to the masses," my father commented after Els concluded her history lesson. "Thad, you should have told her the history that couldn't be found in the books. The unspoken culture."

My jaw tightened. Patrick Kirk Lourie could be unpredictable when he was agitated. He loved a challenge.

Beauty's eyes lit up. "Oh, I would love to know! I mean if that's all right that I know."

"Of course, it's all right for the mate of my son to know." The way he said mate was condescending. I could tell she picked up on it.

Earlier in the night, she asked why I kept referring to her as my mate. I told her it was the equivalent of saying she was my woman. I knew she saw through that answer when she mentioned the meaning of mate based on the biblical word.

"Well, Miss Elsbeth, our tribe is the descendants of wolves." That's all my father said. He didn't give more context around it. There was silence for a moment before he asked her what she thought about that.

Naturally, she looked around confused. "Um, I think that's cool although I'm not sure what that means." She shifted her body to face me. "Thad, can we talk about that later tonight?"

"Yes, Beauty, we can." I leaned over and kissed her lips.

"Let's get you something to eat, so I can get you to my house."

We talked to my parents for a minute more before we walked over to the buffet to make plates. While we were making our plates, Mikayla and Sabastian came over. Sabastian made sure to make an announcement to the pack that Mikayla was off limits. Of course, Enola had something smart to say about him taking a beastless woman serious. With no remorse, he told her to shut the fuck up.

"Hey, I'm going to head to the hotel," Mikayla said. Me and Sabastian looked at each other, then at her.

I scrunched my face. "Why are you staying at a hotel? Cancel that shit. You can stay at my house," I told her. It made no sense for her to waste money on a hotel. "We have a tribe meeting in an hour anyway. You can keep Els busy until I get home."

"That's a good idea. I told you to ask him before you booked the room," Beauty said with delight. "Please stay."

It didn't take much to convince her to stay. When Sabastian told her that he would come over after our meeting, her decision to stay was solidified. Sabastian came with me, Els, and Mikayla to my house to help get them settled, then we headed to the pack meeting. Farad met us at the meeting.

"I heard Enola showed her ass, bro," Farad said as soon as I sat next to him. "She's bogus as hell for that shit. She was talking shit about Els to some of the other girls, but Maggie and Jorie shut her ass all the way down." He chortled. "That shit pissed her off even more."

The huff that left my lungs almost hurt because of the thought of Enola's audacity. "Bro, this is not the first female that she's seen me with. I'm not understanding what the problem is."

Sabastian tittered. "Thad, you act like you didn't bring a woman that no one has ever met to the campfire gathering and introduce her as your mate. Yeah, she may have seen you with other females, but I can guarantee that she has never experienced that shit right there. The second Els and Mi got out of that car, everyone in the pack was like *who dis for*."

"Fuck all that. How your dad take the news?" Farad asked. That was the million-dollar question.

I looked toward the front of the room where my father sat next to Ahote, his spiritual advisor and Enola's father. "I can't really call it. He said a couple smart things to me, but he wasn't overly rude to my baby. At the end of it all, what can he do? Elsbeth is mine and that's what it is and what it's going to be."

"I hear you, brother. I'm happy for you." Farad genuinely spoke. I loved that he always supported me. "Hell, Sabastian, I'm thinking I should give you I'm happy for you too."

Sabastian actually blushed. "Man, there's something about her that speaks to me. I'm gonna chill and see what she's about."

My father started the meeting before we could finish our conversation. It was our run of the mill meeting like it normally was. Luckily, the pack hunted a few weeks prior, so we didn't need to hunt for a while. This was shaping up to be a short meeting. I was ready to get back to my woman.

"All right, everyone. Let's wrap this up. Before we leave, I want to make an announcement," my father said. His smile was eerie. He reached his hand out to my mother who took it and stood by his side. "We want to take this time to announce the engagement of my son Thaddeus and Enola."

I jumped up from my seat. "The fuck you do!" He had me fucked up.

My ma snatched her hand away from my dad. "The fuck we are." Her inner brows were dipped toward her nose.

My sister jumped from her seat. "What the hell, Daddy? Why are you doing this?"

The pack was looking around with confusion and entertainment. For years there was speculation that we were going to get married, but that shit never meant anything to me. People fared better when they minded their own business.

Enola stood with a goofy smile. "Thaddeus, don't be like that. You know this was always the plan."

My beast was pacing, and I was about to join him. "Enola, you have lost your fucking mind. You in here talking about that was the plan. How was it the plan when you're in love with some nigga in Pembroke? Y'all better stop fucking playing with me. All y'all met my mate tonight."

My father stood resolute in front of the pack. "Son, I can't control what the others in the pack do, but you, I can. I will not allow you to bring some beastless bitch in here and talk about mating her."

I felt my body propel forward, but was stopped by Farad, Sabastian, and Oscar. "Aye, man, calm down. Just calm down."

I was trying to get to my father. "Don't you ever in your life disrespect my fucking mate. You got me fucked up."

My father let out a menacing laugh. "No pack leader in this tribe will be mated with a beastless bitch. You have a decision to make. Which is more important to you?"

He wanted to die at the hands of his son. That was the only conclusion that I could come to that he felt so comfortable to continue to call Els a beastless bitch. The beastless part I didn't care about, but that bitch part was about to have him in hospice care.

"Patrick, you are going too damn far. Thaddeus is free to mate whoever he wants. You have no say in that. You are wrong for all of this!" my ma shouted. Our family shit played out in front of the entire pack.

I didn't have shit to make. I calmed down so that my beast would follow my lead. "There is no decision to make. You can have this pack leader shit if it means not being with my mate. You can remove me as a leader, but you can't remove me from the pack or tribe so fuck you."

With shrugged shoulders, my father said, "So be it. Farad, you are the new pack leader. Meeting dismissed."

This dude walked out like it wasn't an issue. He was so stuck on our line being pure when the shit wasn't pure to begin with. The Lourie line was mixed with African Americans who didn't have anything to do with wolves. That's where our rich chocolate skin came from. Our black genes were so strong after years, people still didn't believe some of us had any Native American blood in us. There were non-wolves in our tribe that were not originally in our tribe.

Farad stood there frozen for a second. "Fuck no! I don't want that shit. Thaddeus is the leader of this pack."

"Nah, Farad, you good, bro. If anyone, I would want it to be you." I looked around the room a final time before I went to my mother who stood there with tears in her eyes. "It's all right, Ma. I'm going home to be with my mate." I made sure I said that last part loud enough for my father to hear.

My mother took me into her arms and kissed the tip of my nose like she did when I was a child. "Son, I'm going to come over tomorrow so we can talk. I love you."

I told her that I loved her also, then headed toward the front door. We had our meeting in the community center on the reservation. The community center was five minutes away from my house, but I'd make it home in two with the way I was feeling.

"Thaddeus, can we talk?" Enola's voice came from behind me. "I know you want to get home to your *mate*, so I'll make it short."

I took a deep breath with my head tilted back and eyes closed. Once I had myself together, I turned to face her. I invaded her personal space, putting my face close to hers. My fangs popped out and I let out a guttural growl. Fear registered in her eyes which was what I wanted. "Stay the fuck away from me, bitch. If you come near me or my mate, I won't think twice about making you a bear snack."

My car hadn't turned over before my sister was in my mind. *"Thad, are you all right? Where are you?"*

"I'm good, Sis. Fuck that nigga." There were so many emotions that sat heavy on my chest that I'd never experienced. The one that was the heaviest was hurt. My father had done a lot of questionable things, but this was past that. This was flat out disrespectful. *"I'm going home to be with Els."*

"Thaddeus, I know you don't want to hear this. I think you need to tell her before she leaves tomorrow about what happened and why it happened," my sister urged. *"You want to get in front of this. She's your mate and although it's not official, you still need to interact with her like it is."*

I knew she was right. Now with my father acting crazy and Enola jumped on his bandwagon, I didn't want them to blindside my baby. *Fuck!* I wanted to be able to tell her on my time, but now I was pushed into a corner to tell her. *"I know, Sis! Will you come over in the morning for support?"*

"Baby bro, I'll be there, and I'll even cook breakfast. Now let me go so I can go see a man about a horse."

The fuck! "I don't want to hear that nasty shit. I kill horses!" We both laughed at my assertion before she closed her mind door.

I knew this was something that needed to be done. Fear took over me at the thought of her leaving when she found out. Would she accept me for the gift that the gods bestowed to me? Please let her accept me for who I am.

Elsbeth

"Girl, you know I'm down to jump the fuck out that granola looking bitch," Mi blurted. "Quaker needs to sue her ass for trademark or copyright infringement. There is no way she's around here with their flaky product on her face like that."

My side hurt because I laughed harder than I wanted to. Mi's face held genuine concern like she cared about that girl Enola having adult acne. She wasn't an ugly female, but that acne was tough to see. "Why are you like this? Who says someone looks like granola?"

"I do because that's what the fuck she looks like." She held up the box of chewy chocolate chip granola bars that she ordered in our grocery order that we had delivered tonight. "Why do you think I ordered these? Her face had me craving these shits."

Earlier tonight when Thad brought us to his house, it was absent of food. I gave him a serious side-eye. How was he surviving here? He told me that he spent more time at his condo in Raleigh than here, so when he was here, he ate at his parents or sister's house. He left money for groceries.

We sat in his den in our pajamas watching television. I loved being with my best friend, but I couldn't wait until my man got home. Thad and I hadn't been together for a long time, but the experience was interesting. One thing that was noticeable about my man was his protectiveness and obsessive nature. When we're out in public, if a man looked at me for longer than Thaddeus deemed necessary, he did this sexy growl. The first time he did it, I was turned on more than I've ever been in my entire life. Most women would have seen that as a red flag, but I saw it as a green flag to give him the pussy for the first time.

The first time that we had sex, I concluded that I had been doing it wrong all of my life. That growl was sexier when he was in this pussy. I wasn't a shy or inexperienced girl when it came to sex. I took pride in learning how to please and be pleased.

It made me think about my college boyfriend that I thought was the best that I ever had. I was so in love with that fool. Tony and I were together our entire collegiate career. I knew we were going to get married after we graduated, but he had other plans. He broke up with me after the graduation party that my parents threw me. His parents were also there. Everyone was taken aback when he didn't propose.

The excuse that he gave was that our lives were going in two different directions, and he didn't want to hold me back. I was devastated. Imagine my surprise when a month later, I found out he was engaged to a girl who went to a school a state over. I was pissed because that meant he cheated on me. When I ran up on her like the immature, hurt woman I was at the time, she was very gracious. She said nothing to me.

Later that day, I received an email where my bubble

was further burst. The email explained that Tony and she had been together since high school. When they went to college, they agreed to take a break to have their fun, but they always planned to get engaged after graduation. She went on to tell me that the only reason Tony was with me was because I was beneficial to him. See, Tony wasn't too damn bright which left me to do ninety-seven percent of his schoolwork. As quiet as it was kept, his degree should have had my name on it. There were times that I locked myself in my room to do both of our work.

Mikayla hated him, rightfully so. I didn't want to believe Tony's fiancée, but she provided a paper trail of screenshot conversations between the two of them as well as a group chat with him and his friends. She confirmed that the entire time they were in college, he never fucked with her and was faithful to me, but he was only with me for the reason she proved. She was even in her own relationship that she dissolved a week before graduation.

I was pissed, hurt, and vengeful. I made them think that I bowed out but fuck that. My plan was put in motion. I stayed close to Tony's parents who talked way too much. They claimed to be none the wiser about Tony's plan to break up with me. I wasn't so sure. They told me every graduate school that he applied to.

I made it my business to reach out to every school to provide them with evidence that all of his papers were paid for and completed by another student. How was I able to do that? Well, when we were in a relationship, I joked about offering my paper writing services to others to make money. Tony claimed he wanted to keep my expert services to himself. When he needed a paper, he would jokingly send me a request for the paper, and I would send him a price. I had all of those messages which I provided for the universities. Needless to say, he didn't get accepted by any of them.

He knew I did it because the schools reached out to him with the claims and evidence. Tony ran up on me in an aggressive way. Well, that ended up with my father's gun shooting him in a more aggressive way. Was I wrong, fuck yeah! Do I regret it, fuck no! Fuck him and his now what I know to be mediocre dick. I had Thad to thank for that.

"Aye, why it smells like rose petals in my house?" Thad's voice sounded from the front door. I smelled him before I saw him.

When he came into view, I started to get up to greet him. Before I could, he plopped down next to me, then laid his head on my lap. Something was wrong. "Baby, are you all right?"

"Yeah, the meeting was a lot," he said. "I was ready to get home to you." He looked up at me from my lap. "I'd love if I could do this shit every night."

His ass had been talking about me moving in for a week now. "Baby, we just got together, and you already want me to move in," I said through giggles. "I think that's a little fast."

"Beauty, I would have asked you to marry me already if I didn't think you'd run for the hills," he said with a matter of a fact tone. "I don't have time to be climbing mountains to drag your ass back down, so I said I'd give that some time." With a cheeky smirk, he said, "I'm considerate like that."

Mi snickered. "You better tell my best friend what she has to look for. Now, where is Sabastian so I can get the hell out of y'all's face?"

Thad didn't answer right away. Eventually, he told her that he was on his way now. Not sure how he knew that.

"Baby, let's go to bed so Mi and Sabastian can have

some privacy," I suggested. I wanted some alone time with my man and some dick. Plus, I could feel his energy wasn't up for company.

He didn't say anything as he lifted his head from my lap, then got up. After he helped me up, we retired to his bedroom. I took a shower shortly after I arrived tonight, but he prepared himself for a shower. I went back and forth about whether I should join him. I decided against it. He looked like he needed a minute alone.

Since we'd been together, this was the first time that I felt his energy in a downtrodden state. That bothered me because I wasn't sure why, therefore, I didn't know how to make it better. I relaxed in the bed and strolled on social media until he came back into the room.

"Baby, come here," I requested. "Something is off about you. I don't like it."

He still had the towel around his waist with water trailing down his bare chest. That didn't stop him from climbing in the bed with me. As soon as he was comfortable, his head went back to my lap and his arms wrapped around my legs.

He tilted his head up. "I'm just tired, Beauty. I'm happy you're here."

"Well, are you too tired to dig in this pussy?" My enchanting tone had me wanting to fuck me. *I'm such an amazing person.*

His lids rose high. He hopped up with the most energy. "Shit, I'm never too tired to be in that Red Bull pussy."

I chortled heartedly when he dropped the towel, but it was short lived. I wanted to grab my camera and tape the amazement in front of me. I'd never witnessed a dick physically get hard. When he pulled his towel from his body, his dick was laying comfortably on his thigh. I watched it slowly expand and lengthen. Then in slow motion, it rose like Lazarus.

I scooted to the edge of the bed closest to him. I'd never seen a dick that just needed to be sucked. My nigga was sexy as fuck with his chocolate skin. With my finger, I called him to me.

"What you wanna do with this, Beauty?" His feet slowly brought his dick closer to me. "You gonna suck it for me?"

The answer to his question was my mouth wrapped around the shaft of his dick and the tip of it tickling the back of my throat. His head fell back, and his hand went to the back of my head. His other hand roamed down the front of my body, found my right breast, then gripped it. A moan of satisfaction left my pit. The second his fingers surrounded my nipple and pinched it, my first orgasm of the night welcomed itself.

"Use that hand to play with that pussy. Beauty, don't touch my dick," he grumbled. "You know ya man likes that no hands shit."

That he did. Like a good slut, my right had went to my body flower and my other went to my left breast to massage the nipple. It would be a shame for my right breast to have all the fun. Thad's hand held my head in place, then his hips thrusted forward. Once I was comfortable, the humming started.

"Fuck, fuck, fuck, Beauty!" The humming threw Thad's thrust off for a second, but he gained his composure. "Shit, give me a second and I'll name the song."

This was a little game that I introduced to him. The vibrations from humming on a dick brought most men ultimate satisfaction. I decided that I would test out different songs to evaluate the satisfaction it brought to him. It was his job to guess the song that I hummed. So far, we have only played the game maybe twelve times. *I love sucking his dick.*

He got himself together while I continued to hum. "Shit, some' Mama Patti sang." After I shook my head, he guessed again. "Gladys fucking Knight."

The chuckle on his dick gave a different kind of vibration altogether. Why he continued to name these older singers was comical. I shook my head on his dick.

For another few minutes, he guessed everything from Aretha Franklin to Beyonce to Floetry. "Beauty, I'm about to explode!" He pushed his hips forward. "Muthafucka!"

The warmth of his cum made my wall flower bloom and give away her own fragrant reward. *I love swallowing his little family.* After I made sure he was drained, I pulled back to clean the corners of my lips. All cleaned up, I slid back on the bed. I made sure he had a good view of my body flower. *There it goes again.* His dick assumed the position I loved.

He climbed on the bed after my back lay on it. Thad's hand cuffed under my right leg and pushed it back. Our lips collided as he smoothly slid into me. My oxygen supply was temporarily suspended from the feeling of him stretching me past what felt like my body flower's limit. Thaddeus had the kind of dick that made you want to never do a Kegel again because extra tight pussy was the mistress of devil's dick.

"Th-Thad, baby," I said through a moan. "How does it feel like you're bigger than you were the last time we fucked? That was last night." My body convulsed to the release of my nut.

His lips came to my ear. "It's that wolf dick, Beauty." The growl after his words caused another orgasm that I wasn't ready for.

"Well, fuck me, Mister Wolf. Fuck me!" I damn near begged. Everything about this man was perfect. I didn't know what I'd done to deserve the honor of being his, but I would show gratitude every second.

For the rest of the night, we fucked each other into oblivion. There were parts of the night that I considered telling him that he should work at a stretch studio. The way my muscles relaxed after certain positions was therapeutic. This man could have my pussy or mouth whenever he wanted. We'd have to work up to the ass with that wolf dick.

The Next Morning...

Vitamins might be in my future. It never failed that I was exhausted after we fucked. My arms stretched over my head. I didn't feel a body next to me which prompted me to turn my head. My exhaustion wasn't the only thing that I noticed. *It's nine-thirty in the morning.*

"Good morning, sleepy head." Thad's voice caught my attention. He looked so good in his black sweatpants and wifebeater. "I wanted you to get some rest before I came to wake you."

After I sat up in the bed, he climbed on it to give me a kiss. "Give me another one," I demanded after the first.

"So fuckin' demanding with your sexy ass." Thad shook his head with a titter, but those lips came to mine. "Go take a shower. There's a house full of people here for breakfast."

That made me jump slightly. "What? Is your mom and dad here? I didn't bring anything really cute for me to wear."

I loved his mother Mrs. Parie, but his dad I didn't care

for. He wasn't mean to me last night or anything, but I heard the condescension in his tone when we talked. When I talked, he would glare over at Thaddeus with this look of disgust. I honestly think something happened between him and his father last night at their meeting or whatever it was. That was the reason for his depressive attitude last night.

"No, my dad isn't here. My mom, Farad, Rummie, and Sebastian are here," he told me. "Rummie's cooking, so you better get up. Her ass rarely cooks for anyone."

That had me moving because he was right. Rummie cooked when me, her, Mi, Maggie, and Jorie had a girls' night over a week ago. Some of the best cooking that I'd ever had. "You don't have to convince me to move when Rummie is doing the cooking."

Thad's head bucked back. "You don't move that fast for me." After I insisted that I did, he said, "Let me say it like this. You don't move this fast for me when my dick isn't involved."

My shoulders lifted before I moved to the bathroom. I was not going to talk back to the truth. That dick had me in my car behind the pharmacy during lunch getting fucked. I knew there were cameras back there, but the dick had me not caring. "I'll be out in a few minutes."

It took me longer in the shower, thanks to a certain someone who decided to join me. After amazing shower sex, we were finally in his dining room eating. I was very surprised that he had a dining room with a table and everything. He told me that it came with the house because his mother knew he would never buy one, so she made sure one was there when he moved in.

"Rummie, this food is good! I might have to have you do my weekly meal prep," I told her after a bite of the omelet she made me.

Thad leaned his forearms on the table from his seat in front of me. "You know if you lived here, you could just go two doors down to eat. That would be so convenient. Plus, the pharmacy wouldn't be too far away either."

"This man is planning y'all whole future," Mi said with a giggle. "I like it. I like it a lot."

Sabastian glanced at her. "Keep giggling and you're going to be moving on the reservation before she does." His brow was lifted with the corner of his lip.

What the hell kind of night did they have? My curiosity was piqued. Me and my girl had a lot to talk about.

"Y'all just being all subliminally nasty in front of me," Mrs. Parie said with her nose scrunched up. "I know y'all grown, but y'all not growner than me."

We all laughed. Mrs. Parie gave a light snicker before she stopped. The look she gave Thad caused his laughter to stop. *What is that about?* Eventually all the laughter at the table stopped. The vibe suddenly became serious.

"Beauty, I wanted to talk to you about something," Thad said softly. His tone didn't make me feel like I would like whatever he wanted to talk about. Plus, if he wanted to have this conversation in front of everyone, he must have felt he needed backup for some reason.

My head swiveled toward Mi who gave me a dumb-founded look. I guess she didn't know anything either. "Oh, okay. Is something wrong?"

"No, there's nothing wrong," Thad quickly said waving his hand. That was a relief. "I wanted to talk to you about something that my father told you last night."

I thought about everything that we talked about last night. Thad's father barely spoke outside of when he told me about the history of the tribe. "Are you talking about the tribe history? That's really the only thing that he spoke about."

Thad shifted in his seat. "Yeah, it is. Do you remember what he told you?"

"Yeah, he said your tribe was descendants of wolves," I responded. "Is that what you're talking about?"

He nodded his head. "Yes, that's what I'm talking about." He paused then glanced at his mother. "How do you feel about that?"

Confusion etched my expression. "How do I feel about the old wives' tale of your tribe lineage? I mean cool. My family is descendants of crackheads." I shrugged my shoulders. "Thank God everything doesn't get passed down."

Mi leaned forward with laughter. "Why are you so stupid?" She looked at Thad, then said, "She's not lying though."

Farad stifled his laughter, but Thad didn't even break a smile. Mine dropped quickly. "Is there something else I should have taken from what he said, Thaddeus?"

"Nah, you should have taken it exactly how he said it. My tribe is descendants of wolves. Elsbeth, it's not a wives' tale. It's the truth of what and who we are." His tone was steady and strong. There was no sense of humor in anything that he said.

I sat there silent for a second because what the hell was going on right now. "So, what you're saying is what? You're a wolf, is that what you're saying?"

He looked between his mother, sister, Farad, and Sabastian. After he refocused back on me, he nodded. "That's exactly what I'm saying."

I peeked at my best friend to see if I could read her mind. It didn't take long to know that her thoughts matched mine when she erupted into laughter. "What the fuck y'all got going on?" she asked. "Is this a scare the non-Indian girls joke or some shit?"

"Right, like what the actual hell?" I joined in with Mi. "We're having breakfast with the wolfpack, sis. It must be their motorcycle club." Farad and Thad owned motorcycles.

This was the craziest shit that I'd ever been involved with. "Thad, you're late for the whole April Fool's thing." I pointed at all of his people. "All of y'all decided to be in on this?"

Mrs. Parie leaned forward. "Elsbeth, baby, it's not a joke. What Thaddeus is telling you is real." She glanced down the table. "We are wolves, baby, not a bike club, but wolves."

This was getting weirder by the moment. Now that Mrs. Parie had chimed in, I didn't know how to respond. She didn't come across like a person who joked a lot. The entire mood of the room was extremely tight and serious.

"Okay, well if y'all are wolves, show us," Mi demanded before she crossed her arms over herself, then leaned back in her chair. "I ain't never seen a wolf and y'all telling us all of you are wolves or just like some of you."

"We're all wolves," Sabastian confirmed. It was interesting that a lot of people in this tribe had a darker skin tone than what you would think a person of Native American descent would have. It was like melanin was seeping all up and through the tribe.

Mi's head bucked back. "Oh, you would tell me something like that after you've been all up and through me." She closed her eyes. "I blame my ass for being whorish."

"Mi, shut the hell up," Sabastian roared before he pushed his seat back and stood. "You talk a lot of shit, but let's see if you can handle it when you get what you asked for." He looked at everyone, then said, "Let's go!"

Thad chuckled, then said, "Damn, this was supposed to be about me and my woman. Mikayla done pissed this man off." He stood from his seat. "Let's go, Beauty."

Thad walked around the table, stood next to me, then extended his hand. There was a desperation laced in his expression. It caused me to put my hand in his. I had no idea what I was walking into, but I wanted to find out.

We all walked through the house to the back deck. Thad's house was gorgeous, and the deck was the things great party decks were made of. When we got on the deck, Thad instructed me and Mi to stay on the deck. Sabastian opened the screen door and led everyone else into the backyard.

"Damn, I'm surprised you didn't flip the table over when Sabastian yelled at you." My voice was low when I spoke to Mi. "Let me find out wolf dick got you quiet," I joked.

Her neck snapped in my direction. "Girl, fuck you," she mumbled with a titter. "You got jokes about wolf dick, but you been getting supposed wolf dick. I just got some." She waved me off then shouted into the yard, "Y'all talking about wolves but all I see is a bunch of folks standing around."

The mention of wolf dick brought my mind back to last night when Thaddeus and I were having sex. *It's that wolf dick, Beauty.* Wow!

"Beauty, I don't want you to be scared, okay? I'm not going to come onto the porch unless you want me to after I shift," Thad informed. He glanced at his mother, sister, and Farad who stood near each other. "Ma, Rummie, and Farad, y'all don't shift. Only Sabastian and I will."

After they agreed, Thad and Sabastian started removing their clothing. I watched with anticipation of the unknown.

Both left their boxer briefs on. Mi grabbed my hand, then leaned into me. "Oh, I see why you talking about wolf dick," she said in a whisper.

I didn't want to laugh, but I couldn't help it. "Bitch, I see a wolf dick—"

Both of our humorous demeanors went to hell when we saw two fine ass men turn into two scary, big ass wolves. Based on the slight wetness trickling down my leg, I peed a little bit. Where Thaddeus stood was now a big, black, shiny coat wolf. Thad's eyes were brown, but this wolf's eyes were a grayish, green.

I stood there frozen as the wolf looked at me for a second, gave a low whimper, then lowered his head before he did his body. Where Sabastian stood was a brown wolf. I couldn't describe it any more than that because I was focused on what was standing in Thad's place.

"Oh, fuck no!" Mi's voice jolted me back into reality. *Wait, everything is the same!* She didn't jolt me anywhere because I was already in a reality that I didn't understand. "Let's go!" She abruptly pulled me through the back door before she closed and locked it. "Get your bag so we can go."

I rushed to Thad's bedroom and grabbed my purse. Fuck those clothes and other shit. By the time I was coming out of his room, Rummie was coming down the hallway. I stopped in my tracks. "Are you one of them too?"

Rummie held both of her hands up in surrender. "I am. We will not hurt you, Elsbeth. I know you don't believe that we will."

"Just let me leave please. We... We won't tell anyone." I'd never been a person to be afraid of anyone, but this was a different situation. I wasn't evenly matched to a fucking big ass wolf. "You'll never see us again."

Rummie's expression softened. "Els, that's not what we want, love. My brother very much wants to see you again, and again, and again. He wants you to accept him for all of him, so you know exactly who you're going to love and who loves you."

"Els, let's go! Fuck all that shit." Mikayla yelled from behind Rummie. "Get the fuck out of her way."

Rummie once again threw her hands up with a smirk and stepped out of my way. I rushed past her, but not without her grabbing my wrist. A sudden calmness came over me. "We'll see each other again," Rummie said softly. I heard her voice, but I didn't see her lips moving.

"I'on know if y'all immune to bullets. We gonna find out if you don't let her go, Rummie." The sound of Mikayla's gun cocked was the next thing heard.

When Rummie released my wrist, the panic seeped back in. My feet double stepped to Mi, and we were out of the house, inside of her car, and pulled out of the driveway in less than three minutes. We rode in silence for most of the trip until Mi broke it. "Did that really just happen?"

"I don't know what the fuck I just saw. I mean, I know but I never thought I would ever see something like that. What are we, in a Stephenie Meyers book?"

Mi was talking a mile a minute, but I was too confused to talk. I couldn't comprehend any of it, and what's more, I didn't want to. Twenty minutes before we got home, my phone started to buzz. I knew it was Thad because I'd given him a specialized vibration. Against my better judgment, I looked at my phone screen. The phone needed to be unlocked before I was able to see the message. Once it was unlocked, I went to the message thread.

My Bae: Beauty, please just talk to me.

My Bae: I know U need time. I'm gonna give U that but I'm not going anywhere.

My heart pulled at me. I liked him, I really liked him. He'd engrained himself into my life on every level in such a short time. When I told my parents that we were testing out a relationship, my father started calling him son. My father never called my ex-boyfriend son the entire time that we were together. Hell, he barely talked to the boy at all.

"Best friend, why are you crying?" Mi asked. Until she asked, I hadn't realized that I was crying. "Did he say something crazy?" She looked at my phone in my hand.

"No, he didn't say anything crazy." I told her what the text said. She asked me if I was going to respond. I thought about my answer and said the only thing I knew to say in the moment. "I'm going to tell him to leave me the hell alone."

Me: Leave me alone. I want nothing to do with U.

The bubbles started bubbling. I sat on pins and needles watching them. What was he going to say? Would he say fuck me, like I was pretty much saying to him?

My Bae: Beauty, I'll give you time to swallow this. We'll get together and talk about this and how we WILL move forward. Be safe Elsbeth.

I was not going to go back and forth with him, so I blocked him. That was the end of that. Why would God do this to me? He sent me the perfect man who was a wolf. What the hell was that? Right now, all I needed was a bottle of wine, a bath, and my bed.

Thaddeus

A Little Time Later...

My mind was completely fucked up. I needed my woman, but she wasn't fucking with me right now. I'd been staying in Raleigh since the reveal because I wanted to be close to Elsbeth. I left her alone for a week to let her calm down. After that week, I was on her ass. The fear that flashed in her eyes when she saw me come into the pharmacy to deliver the mail almost broke my heart. This was the woman that I loved. Yeah, I loved her ass.

What I needed was for Elsbeth to not fear my beast. I knew that was a hard concept because there were women in the pack that feared my wolf. Male werewolves were bigger than the female werewolves and both were bigger than regular wolves. How was I going to get a human to not fear my beast?

Elsbeth changed her work schedule to a later shift. It took me another week to figure out that she changed her shift. I guess she thought if it was late enough that I would miss her when I brought the mail to the pharmacy. Joke was on her ass, because I was going to bring that mail when the fuck I felt like it.

Mikayla still worked most of her original shifts, so I saw her when I went in. Her mean ass would say slick shit, but not too much. Sabastian had her ass in a chokehold. Yeah, I wasn't sure if Mikayla told her best friend that four days after the reveal, she was back on my boy Sabastian. I wasn't hating at all. I just wished my woman could get over it as quickly as Mikayla did.

Today was the second day that I saw Beauty at work. Her ass blocked my phone number, but she didn't block me on social media. The reels that I still sent on a consistent basis were seen although she never responded to them. The fact that she watched them and hadn't blocked me there told me a lot. I still had a chance.

"Aye, Thaddeus! How you doing, young man?" Mr. Bill greeted me as soon as he saw me. He was a cool dude.

Elsbeth's head popped up quickly with her eyes widened. She was so damn beautiful. Her locs set atop her head. Today she wore her glasses which she rarely wore. My beast groaned loudly within me. If I didn't know any better, I would have thought that someone could have heard him.

"Mr. Bill, I'm good! How was your vacation?" He'd gone on vacation and his son stepped in while he was gone. "You and your wife must have had a grand time. You look relaxed as hell, my man."

He whipped himself down like he was a young dude. "You know, I'm trying to stay cool out here and keep my woman happy." He took the mail that I extended to him. "Elsbeth, you can take a fifteen to talk to your man."

The benefit of him being on a damn near month long vacation was that he was oblivious about what was going on between us. He patted me on my shoulder before he headed back behind the counter. Els was about to say something to him, but he answered the phone before she could.

"Come here, Beauty. Let me talk to you, baby." I looked at her with soft eyes. Fear was not something that I wanted her to have when I was in her presence.

She hesitated as she looked between me and Mr. Bill. My baby wasn't a person that liked drama, especially when it involved her. She slowly walked toward me and stopped just short of being within my arm's reach.

"Beauty, we can talk right here. We don't have to go anywhere," I let her know. She needed to feel safe, and I would never take that from her.

She shook her head slowly. "No, we can go in the back." She sounded unsure of herself. I didn't like that at all.

I took small steps toward her. When I was close enough, my hand gently grabbed her. Her body jerked so I pulled my hand back. "Baby, we don't have to go anywhere."

She frantically looked around the pharmacy. As I knew, the front cashier was zoomed into our interaction. "No, we can go in the back. I don't want people in our business."

She walked past me toward the back of the pharmacy, then out the back door where we usually talk or fuck. I was sure to keep a comfortable distance from her when we got outside. The sound of my rapid beating heart drowned out the noise of the outside. "I miss you, Beauty."

The only thing that I saw was the top of her bun because of her lowered head. There was silence, too much damn silence. "Beauty, I love you. Do you know that?"

Finally, she lifted her head. "You, you can love?" Her question confused me more than the realization that she was serious about it.

"What do you mean, can I love? Of course I can,

Beauty. I love you," I calmly said. "I'm still a man. I under-stand that my beast is confusing to you, but it's something that I can't control. It's something the gods blessed me with." Yes, I wanted her to be all right with me, but I would not be ashamed of my beast.

The gravel moved around as she shuffled her feet on it. I watched her fingernail dig into her arm. "Thad, I really like you, but I don't know. I never... I don't know." The wetness in her eyes made me move closer to her.

"Can I just hug you?" I asked. "All I want right now is to hug you, Beauty. I miss you." I wasn't sure if she needed me, but I damn sure needed her. I was man enough to know and admit that.

The first tear fell just before she nodded in acceptance. My hand gently took hers to pull her into my arms. I cocooned her into my chest. She sobbed into my chest. My lips kissed the top of her earlobe. "Beauty, I love you. My beast loves you."

That's all I knew to say. Ma told me to be consistent with my love but try not to be overbearing. I wasn't sure if this was what she meant. All I knew was that I needed her in me and my beast's life.

"I don't know what to think, Thaddeus," she cried into my chest. "What does it mean that you're a wolf?" She pulled back from the hug. *She's about to ramble.* "I mean, I know what it means. I saw it. Like I never knew stuff like that was real. You're a real animal.

"A big wolf that could kill me." As if she just realized I had the capability to kill her, she jumped back. "Oh my God! Would you kill me?"

I put my hand up. "No, Beauty, I love you. I would never hurt you nor would my beast." I smiled softly. "Els-beth, my beast loves the fuck out of you."

For a second, I thought to tell her that my beast was the main reason I was able to protect her in that situation that could have changed the trajectory of her life in a detrimental fashion, but I thought better of it. To call that out would have been manipulative in the most heinous of ways. She was still trying to heal, and I would never use it to my advantage.

She stared at me for a beat. With her finger she wiped a fallen tear from her cheek. "Can... Can I have some time to think about this?"

That wasn't what I wanted. "Beauty, I don't want to give you too much time. Can you unblock my number so I can at least get in touch with you to check in?" When she didn't respond, I said, "Elsbeth, I'm trying to be reasonable. I don't have to have a beast to be a beast about you, Beauty."

She rolled her beautiful eyes, pulled her phone from her scrub pocket, then tapped the screen. Seconds later, she said, "You're unblocked." She tried to hide the small, smirky smile, but failed miserably.

There might be more hope for us than I originally thought. I pulled my phone out of my short cargo pocket, pulled up her contact, then sent her a text.

Beauty Love: I love U

When the *delivered* notice showcased under the text, I smiled. "Thank you, Beauty. I'm gonna get back to my route. Text me when you get home to let me know you're safe."

"Fine, Thaddeus," she quipped before she moved to walk past me to get to the back door. I watched her walk into the back door. What she mumbled under her breath that I was sure she didn't know I heard, made me smile.

My boyfriend is a fucking wolf. Yeah, that's right. He sure the fuck is.

A Short Time Later...

"I'm trying to find out how Els's ass doesn't know that her sneaky ass best friend is over here like she is," I fussed. Yeah, I was lowkey hating because of how much time Mikayla was spending here as of late.

I was still being patient as fuck with Beauty, but she was about to have me on her ass. Since our short conversation at the pharmacy, we had begun exchanging reels again. I sent her four before she returned one. Once she returned that one, she knew what the fuck that meant. *We're in a real relationship*. When I texted Beauty, she responded. She also turned her location back on allowing me to have access to it.

Sabastian guffawed. "Man, I don't ask my stink about a conversation she has with her best friend," he said. "All I know is that when she wants to come or I want her to come, she does."

We were at my condo in Raleigh chilling after Mikayla left Sabastian's house. "Your stink? Really, your grown ass calling that girl stink?" I knew that was his nickname for her and it was hilarious.

Sabastian, much like me, was a man that fell hard and fast. That could be a double-edged sword. It worked against him with his son's mother. I hoped it worked out better with Mikayla. "That green doesn't look good on you. I can't wait for Elsbeth to fully fuck with your hating ass again."

This week had been hell because my father was on his good bullshit. He called a meeting with the pack to make the change of leadership official. Farad wanted nothing to do with being the pack leader although I told him that I wanted him to take the position. If I had to be in a pack with a leader that wasn't me then I wanted it to be him. He said it was the principle of the thing, so my father could kiss his ass. Farad was on his way here now after spending time with his girl, Jorie. That was a newfound relationship that we all knew was going to happen.

Like he heard me thinking about him even with my mind closed, he came bopping into my house. "What's up, y'all?" If he smiled any harder, his cheeks would have touched his ear.

"Damn, Jorie got you smiling like that, my man?" Sabastian asked with a smile of his own. *All these in love fuckas.*

Farad went to my kitchen, then came in the den with a beer in his hand. "Fuck yeah, she does. I should have been messing with her, but you know how that goes. Letting fuck boys get in my head."

"What you mean, you let fuck boys get in your head?" Sabastian asked. "I know you're not around here letting people keep you from your happy. I know that's not what you were doing."

Farad dropped his shaking head. He lifted it with a chuckle. "Man, you know dudes around here hate on Jorie just like they hate on Rummie. It never bothered me, but I had to make sure my shit was right before I stepped to her."

"So, you're the fuck boy that had to get out of your own head?" I inquired. Based on his statement, it sounded to me like that was the case. He was his own fuck boy.

Farad waved me off. "Whatever! You know what I mean." He set his beer down, then lit his blunt. "I heard Elsbeth has been talking to Rummie."

I choked on the beer that I'd just drank. That was news to me. "What you mean you heard my sister's been talking to my woman? She hasn't told me shit."

"Well, I mean, I could see her not telling you yet," Farad

casually said. "The only reason I know is because Jorie is on her way to meet them at a bar. If she wasn't going, I'd still be laid up in my place with her."

I pulled my phone out to call my sister, but Sabastian snatched it from me. "Aye, chill, before you fuck yourself up without even trying." He paused for a moment before he continued. "Think about it, dude. If she's willing to physically hangout with the girls then you shouldn't be too far behind. Don't fuck that up because you want to jump the gun."

I knew he was right, but damn. I wanted my baby. "Man, she better be over this shit in the next forty-eight business hours or there's going to be a problem. I'm tired of playing with my mate."

"You serious about that mate shit, huh?" Farad chuckled but nodded his head. "I get it, though, because I'm about to be the same way with Jorie's sexy ass."

Sabastian chortled. "How the fuck are we all in here acting lovesick like some high school boys?" He had a point. None of us had been with our women for a long time, but I knew all three of us would flip the world upside down for these women.

We continued to kick it for the night. Sabastian rarely hung out because of being a single father, but when he could he did. He took his role as a father very seriously. His parents passed away when he was in his twenties before his son was born. He was very particular about who he allowed around his son. My mother, Rummie, Maggie, and Jorie were pretty much the only women in Sabian's life. I wasn't sure if Mikayla had met Sabian yet.

Around eleven o'clock, Sabastian's phone rang. Based on the cheesy ass ringtone, I assumed it was Mikayla. He answered the phone cheerfully, but less than a second after he said hello his forehead wrinkled. Seconds later he touched the screen. "Kayla, why the fuck are you calling me from jail?"

The words from his question echoed in my ear. *The fuck did he mean she's calling from jail?* If she was in jail, where the hell was Beauty? I was already on my feet to get my keys from the key holder. Farad wasn't too far behind me. Sabastian spoke for another few minutes before he disconnected the call. His head went to his hand before he lifted it and stood.

"Rummie, Jorie, Kayla, and Elsbeth were locked up for fighting. They have a hearing at one this morning and will more than likely be released on a PR (personal recognizance) bond since they don't have a record," Sabastian said with glowered eyes.

Farad crossed his arms over his chest. His stance widened. "Who the fuck were they fighting?"

"Enola and her little Egor crew." Sabastian walked toward the front door. "Now this bitch is going way too fucking far. Enola was already far with that shit her and your daddy did. Now she's fucking with my woman."

We all chose to drive separate vehicles. I hoped that Beauty would come back to my place with me, but I knew that was not likely. The biggest detail that stuck out about this situation was Enola and her crew being in a bar in Raleigh. Lumberton was not a small city and there were many restaurants, clubs, bars, and lounges to go to. To my knowledge, she'd never gone to places in Raleigh to hang out. In Lumberton, Enola considered herself a celebrity. Her being the daughter of the spiritual advisor to the chief of our tribe, which was the second most coveted position in the tribe, put her on a pedestal. The same was true for me and my sister being the children of the chief.

Enola loved the attention she got. She never paid for shit when she went out, therefore, in my mind her going out in Raleigh was for a very specific purpose. If it were my guess, it was to fuck with Beauty and Mikayla. She'd seen Mikayla on the reservation when she visited Sabastian just like others had. We got to the courthouse just before one in the morning and we waited in the lobby.

The ladies didn't appear until close to three in the morning. Beauty was the first one to walk out of the door that led to the back. I jumped out of my seat. "Beauty, baby, are you all right?"

There were tears in her eyes. Her feet stopped in front of me. She lifted her finger, then with a subdued tone said, "Ask your fiancée how she's doing. Don't worry about me."

A grimace welcomed itself to my expression. "I don't have a fucking fiancée." My anxiety rose. "If anyone is my fiancée that's your ass, Beauty. Don't fucking play with me."

"Brother, I told her that when Enola said that dumb shit." Rummie rushed over to us. "Thaddeus, I don't know how, but the bitch has an engagement ring and a fucking marriage license with both of your signatures on it."

My ears started ringing. I tilted the ear closest to Rummie toward her. "What the fuck did you just say to me?" There was no way she just said that dumb shit. I heard Sabastian and Farad grumble.

"I don't know how, Thaddeus," Rummie said. "She showed it to Els. She doesn't believe me that it was not real."

Elsbeth looked between the two of us. "Like I said, talk to your bitch ass fiancée. She should be out here in a minute. Stay the fuck away from me."

She stepped to the left where Mikayla stood. Sabastian's arm was around her waist. "Can I use your car to get home? I want you to have time with your man that I didn't know you had until tonight." Hurt sounded in her voice.

A tear fell from Mikayla's eye. "Els, please don't be like that. I can take you home."

"I don't want you to take me home. Go spend time with your man. It's no big deal," Els assured before she held her hand out.

In defeat, Mikayla handed over her car key. Beauty didn't offer any salutations before she stormed out of the building. I followed Beauty out of the building as I called out to her. She ignored the hell out of me. She climbed her beautiful ass into Mikayla's car then drove off.

As if the staff was waiting for us to leave the building, moments later Enola and her crew came out. Enola paused when she saw me with bulging eyes. *Yeah, bitch, look scared.*

I stalked over to her. "Give me the fucking marriage license that you and my father forged now." I didn't need to ask how she forged my name because I already knew.

She crossed her arms over her busty chest. "I don't have a fucking marriage license. I don't know what you're talking about."

My beast was begging to come out to play. It's one thing to fuck with me but fucking with my mate was unforgivable. When my fangs grew, her friend Judy pulled a piece of paper out of her pocket, then extended it to me. Enola's fear of me was minimal and I knew that. She always banked on our history to stop me from hurting her. As far as I was concerned, at this point our past history worked against her because she should know better. I snatched the paper out of Judy's hand.

My blood shot into my eyes seeing my signature forged with a date earlier in the week. "So, this is what you and my father are on? Y'all out here forging documents." She

105

jumped back when I quickly invaded her space. "What the fuck is going on with you? This is not what the hell we do because your ass doesn't even want me on that level. Last time that I checked, you got a nigga that you claim to love."

Her head slowly lowered before her hip popped out to the side. Her expression was soft when she finally focused back on me. "Thaddeus, I thought I loved him. It wasn't until a little while ago that I realized that I loved you and really wanted you," she said with conviction. "I've always loved and wanted to be with you, but we agreed a long time ago to just be friends."

"Bullshit," I responded with a low growl. "Your ass thought you would always have access to me, but now that you don't, you're having a fucking tantrum. When I used to fuck off with these other hos, it never impeded on you getting this dick. Now that I've met my mate, you know it's over for you."

She could play that she just realized she loved me game all she wanted to. I knew she was lying like fuck. As a matter of fact, when I was twenty-seven, I played with the idea of us trying it again. When I came to her about the idea, she literally laughed in my fucking face and told me I was smoking. Enola waved me off.

I only had one more thing to say to her and I was done with her, but I had something for my father. "Look, bitch, stop fucking playing with me. Fucking with my mate is fucking with me and my beast. Enola, when my fangs grow the next time, they're going to get driven into your fucking neck. Let's see if a dead dog can get married."

A deep gasp left her mouth, and her lids expanded. "How dare you threaten me? I will make sure your father and mine know that you are out here willing to lose it all for a bitch that can... ah!"

I lunged toward her but was held back by Sabastian and Farad. "Come on, man. This ditzy broad ain't worth it."

"Shut the fuck up, Sabastian! You would have thought you learned about fucking with those beastless bitches when your ditzy baby mama abandoned you and your son," Enola roared. "I guess not with your dumb ass."

Without warning, Rummie ran up to Enola, then punched her in her face. *Shit, my sis ass is about to get locked back up.* "My brother may not be able to put hands on you, but I'm going to every fucking time I see your ho ass."

Enola was on the ground crying and nursing her already blackening eye. Someone had already busted her lip in the previous fight from what it looked like. I was holding my sister back. "Let's go, Rummie."

She talked shit the entire time I pulled her to the car. "Yeah, bitch! Every time I see you, I'm gonna tap that ass. You fuckin' with the right one."

This shit here! I hated the situation that my father and Enola had put me in. Although I hated it, I was never going to give up on having my mate. Well, I had her, she just needed to know that shit.

A Few Days Later...

I stayed in Raleigh longer than I normally did after the fight incident. I pulled up on my baby and fixed her breakfast a few days ago. She was tripping about the shit asking how I got a key to her house. That was a stupid ass question. When I told her we exchanged keys, she acted like my key wasn't on her keyring. I love my woman and her silliness.

Today was the first time that I'd stepped foot back in Lumberton. I took the time to handle the legal business of getting that bogus marriage license taken care of. I should have pressed charges on Enola and my father, but I digressed. I told Rummie not to say shit to our mother about the marriage license because I wanted to be the one to tell Parie Lourie about her fuck ass husband. I knocked, then walked into my parents' house. I had already called Ma to see where she was.

"Hey, Ma." I greeted when I walked into the den where her and my father were. "How you doing?"

The strife between my father and I was weighing on her heavily. Unfortunately, she was in the middle and would more than likely stay there. I would never ask her to go against her husband, however, wrong was wrong. She made it clear that she didn't agree with his actions at the meeting, but she still stood by her man. I was a grown man, so this wasn't a choose your child over your man situation.

"Son!" she rejoiced at the sight of me before popping up from the couch to hug me tightly. "I've missed you so much. Don't you ever stay away from me this long."

My attention was on my father as I hugged my mother. He was zoned into me just as much as I was zoned into him with his fuck ass. "I'll try not to. You're welcome to come to my house or condo any time you want." I pulled back from the hug. "Patrick, you're of course not invited."

My mother smacked my arm. "Thaddeus Patrick Lourie! I did not raise you to be disrespectful to your father!"

"Parie, why are you surprised? The way you pamper that boy, it's no wonder that he's not a sissy instead of a beastless lover." My father spewed. "No need to reprimand him now."

I took deep breaths while I counted to ten. I wanted to spaz on his ass, but I had to stay focused. "You're funny, Patrick." I pulled the fraudulent marriage license from my back pocket. "Since we're discussing disrespect, Ma, take a look at this." I handed her the license.

She opened the paper, then scanned it. A befuddled expression surfaced to her face. After another minute she looked up at me. "So, you are going to marry Enola?"

"Absolutely not. What you have in your hand is a marriage license that your husband and Enola forged. With a fake ID, Patrick here went down to the courthouse and Bradley Coreton took a nice fee on the side to file it." I glared at my father. "Don't worry, Patrick, Bradley is no longer employed and may be facing criminal charges. I'm not sure how that will play out for you and bitch ass Enola."

My mother's head was on a swivel between me and her husband. "Patrick, how could you? Why the fuck would you do some stupid shit like that knowing he doesn't want to marry that whore?" My mother rarely questioned my father, at least in front of me and Rummie. To see it was refreshing.

My father finally stood up. The entire time since I walked in the door, he seemed unfazed. His wife questioning him got some action from him.

"Ma, it gets better. Enola then took this piece of bullshit and presented it to my mate as if it were legit causing more of a rift between me and her," I informed her. I paused to allow the gravity of the situation to lie in her heart. "The result of that action was Enola getting her ass beat and my girl, Rummie, Mikayla, and Jorie getting arrested."

A tear cascaded down my mother's cheek. In the past, we'd had conversations about things that my father had done during the course of their thirty-four-year relationship that brought her pain. Like a good wife she stuck it out.

Some of those things that brought her pain were a few adulterous affairs that my father felt were no big deal because he only gave the women his dick and not his heart. "You fucking bastard. I knew you were scandalous, but never in all my years would I think that would extend to our children."

My father rushed my mother, causing her to go back into the wall. The paper fell from her hand. The fear in her eyes told me that this was not the first time he'd been aggressive although it was the first time that I'd seen it. "Don't you ever fucking talk to me like that." His voice boomed throughout the den.

Nah, we can't have this. My protective nature took over and my fist went into the side of his head. I took off on his ass like he was a random fuck boy on the street. "Muthafucka, have you lost your fucking mind?"

My father wasn't a slow opponent. My mother yelled for us to stop. She knew what would happen if we didn't. Blows came my way from my father before he stepped back and shifted right there in the den. His shift triggered mine.

"You think you can win this, son?" My father spoke telepathically to me. I noticed he opened his mind to the entire pack. He wanted to make some sort of example of me, but that shit wasn't going to happen.

Without warning, my mother shifted. Now we had three big ass wolves in the den. We tore most of the furniture up just from the shift. When my mother shifted, my father and I paused because she rarely shifted. She slowly stepped in front of me. *"Touch my son and I will kill you, Patrick."* She too gave the pack open access to her mind.

"You dare defy me in front of the pack?" His grimace was bold with his fangs on full display. *"Your disloyalty is showing itself, Parie."*

My mother chortled. *"My disloyalty? Patrick, we can play the game in front of the pack if we want to, but both of us know who the disloyal person in this marriage is,"* she said calmly. *"All of that aside, when you fuck with my children, then you fuck with the devil in me. You and Enola. Enola, darling, do you hear me? I'm coming for you next."*

Right as my mother took a step toward my father, I heard the front door open and hit the wall hard. My head turned to see Rummie, Farad, and Sabastian run in. "Mama, Daddy, what is happening? Stop, please stop!" she said out loud through her tears.

"Get the fuck out of my house!" my mother yelled. *"You are no longer welcomed here."* My mother shifted back to her human form, exposing her naked body. Rummie rushed over with a blanket, then handed it to our mother.

Farad grabbed another blanket with anticipation of my father's shift. Seconds later, the shift occurred. The blanket was handed to my father, and he wrapped it around his waist. "You're putting me out of my house?"

There was a moment of silence that allowed me to shift. Sabastian had a towel ready for me. The tension in the room was solid. A knife couldn't cut through it even if it was a machete.

"Patrick, this is my house, how soon we forget. When we married, my father built this house and the deed is in my name only," she confessed. From the shocked expression, my father never knew that bit of information. "See, my father knew you weren't shit even with the potential of you being the chief. Now like I said..." She stepped into my father's personal space. "Get the fuck out of my house with your disloyal ass."

I'd never seen my father defeated until this day. When he asked my mother where he should go, she told him to go to his whore Chepi's house. I glared at my father before my head snapped in my sister's direction. Chepi was my mother's best friend and our godmother. She was with my mother all the time, so confusion took over.

He looked between all of us. With his communication only open to me, he said, *"You will pay for this, you ingrate."*

He stomped toward the back of the house, but my mother stopped him. "You have clothes at Chepi's house. I'll ensure the rest of your things are sent there by the weekend. Now get the fuck out." She pointed toward the front door.

The growl that left my father's gut got a reaction from Farad. He stepped into my father's space. "You heard her. Get the fuck out."

My father burst into laughter. "I see this is an uprising." He pointed at everyone in the room. "The sun will not rise for your betrayal."

"Take that bullshit out of here!" my mother yelled. She stepped toward him. "You betrayed this family the first time you broke your vows. I wish you long dark nights and rainy days, bastard."

My father looked her up and down before storming out of the house. After my father left and the door was closed, my mother casually turned to us, then asked, "What would you all like me to cook for dinner?" She looked at the clock on the wall. "It's late as hell. Thad, why you come over here after eleven at night?"

"Mama, you're going to act like all of that just didn't happen? Since when has Daddy been messing with Chepi, and why are you still friends with her?" Rummie asked the question we all wanted to know because what the hell!

My mother waved her off. "Girl, that's old news. She's been fucking your father off and on for over twenty-seven years now. At first, I was hurt. I confronted them and they apologized, swearing to never do it again. I forgave, but less than a year later we were back in the same situation with them fucking," she said with a nonchalant shrug. "I wasn't about to keep going back and forth with them, so I let them have at it.

"It didn't matter to me because I had a satisfying affair of my own," she callously admitted. "Now, what y'all want to eat? I don't want to talk about this shit tonight. We can talk tomorrow after I beat Enola's ass so we can have a full story to talk about."

Sabastian and Farad murmured things under their breath. Tonight, I learned more about my parents' marriage then I ever wanted to know. It was one thing to hear that your father had an affair; it was a completely different thing to hear that your mother had one. Apparently, a very satisfying one at that. "Ma, you have the stuff to make succotash?" After she confirmed, I told her to make that because she made it the best.

I told everyone that I was going to take a shower. I was in the shower for about fifteen minutes before I got out, got dressed, and joined the others. When I returned, there was this ominous feeling in the room. "What's wrong with y'all?"

Rummie looked like she'd been crying while Sabastian looked pissed. My mother walked over to me slowly. "Baby boy, we need to go to Raleigh." She stopped for a second. "Elsbeth and Mikayla were attacked earlier tonight. Her mother called Rummie to let her know, so she could tell you."

Elsbeth

Earlier That Night...

'm happy that I got over myself when it came to Mikayla's relationship with Sabastian. I missed her so much during the time that I was mad with her. I wasn't really sure if I was mad at her more than I was mad with myself. I wanted to get over Thaddeus, his family, and friends' confession as quickly as she did. Yes, he was a wolf and in the normal sense of everything, that was unnatural. The conflict was, just because something was unnatural does it make it wrong?

A few days after the fight with that Enola bitch, I called Mikayla. The night that I got home from jail, I changed the code that she had to my apartment. She called my parents like a bratty sister and tattled on me. She didn't tell my mother all of the details, but enough to have her calling me to fuss. That resulted in us sitting down to talk. She had been trying to convince me to talk to Thaddeus since. At this point, I was just being stubborn because I missed the fuck out of my man. He let me know the second that I replied to one of his reels that we were still in a relationship.

"So, remember, we can't get too lit because we riding to see our men after this," Mi reminded me. To my eye roll, she said, "Whatever, bitch! You know you miss that wolf dick."

I hated that her statement made me laugh and rang true. I missed Thad's dick probably more than I missed him. I would never tell him, but he probably would be able to tell the second my body flower gobbled up his dick. "We only having two mixed drinks and a shot at the beginning of the night, then water for the rest."

We were going to a cool ass hookah lounge that had a karaoke night. Mi and I used to go all the time when they first opened. On top of it being fun, they had amazing food. Their tacos were better than most Mexican restaurants that I had been to. "Well shit, let's get it popping!"

"Yes, bitch! Shake that ass!" Mi hyped me up as I shook my ass to the music. "That's my best frien'! That's my Best frien'!"

We were having the time of our lives. We didn't stick to the two mixed drinks and a shot, but such is a fun life. I shook my ass until the song switch over for the next person to sing their song. I'd already sung my heart out to a Brandy and Faith Evans song. "Girl, we gonna have to call our niggas to come get us. It's not looking too good on the driving."

We both chortled before we sat back in our seat. After I told the waitress that I wanted a bottle of water, I relaxed my back on the seat. I loved their seats because they were surprisingly comfortable.

"Bitch, look who the hell I spy over there." Mi smacked my leg hard after she spoke. "Tell me that's not who I think it is."

I zoomed in on what or who she was glaring at. Shakina and Trice. They had their eyes on us. I didn't feel like any bullshit tonight. Shakina already got her ass beat, so I hope her ass chilled for her own safety. "Girl, I'm not thinking about them."

Just as the words rolled off my lips, Shakina stood. Please don't come over here. Please don't come over here. God didn't like me today because she was beelining in our direction. Mi leaned over toward me. "If she come over here with the bullshit, I'm going back to jail with a fucking smile."

I knew she meant what she said, so I started praying. "Hey, Elsbeth." Shakina greeted. She raised her hands to show the palms of them. "I come in peace. I wanted to come over here to apologize." She moved closer to make sure that I could hear her. The music wasn't too loud to not have a conversation, therefore there was no reason for her to get any closer to me.

"You can stay right there," I said holding my hand up to stop her from moving closer. "As far as the apology is concerned, you can keep that. I don't need or want it."

Shakina huffed, looked at Trice, then back at me. Frustration settled on her face. "I understand that you don't need it. For therapeutic reasons, I need and want to give it to you. My therapist thought it was something I should do."

My face contorted. I knew this bitch didn't just say something about therapy. "Girl, you and your therapist are idiots. You went to therapy because you set me up to get raped? Ho, fuck you and that therapy you're in. Get the fuck out of my face." Her impudence was loud.

The tear that left Shakina's eye didn't hide the anger.

"*You know what, that's fine. I did what I could do. I'm at peace with that and that's all that matters.*"

Mi *laughed, then said, "Fuck your peace, ho. I hope every time you feel a Planck length of peace, you get a fucking hangnail, splinter, and a Charlie horse in ya coochie.*"

My head slowly turned to my best friend because what the fuck! There was no smile or smirk present which let us know she was serious as hell. Shakina's friend Trice stood behind her as she desperately tried to suppress her laughter. She failed miserably. Shakina spun around, called her a bitch, then stormed off. Yeah, she better had redirected that anger elsewhere.

"*I don't know why I deal with you. A Charlie horse in her coochie!*" I *burst into uncontrollable laughter.* "*I hate you sometimes.*"

Mi *flipped her hair over her shoulder.* "*You deal with me because you love me. It's always loyalty over love.*"

My face scrunched. "*Bitch, if it's loyalty over love, then why did you go back to fucking with Sabastian?*" I *was fucking with her, and I hope she knew it from the smile on my face.*

"*Girl, you were mad at Thad not Sabastian. It was fuck Thad all day. Sabastian was my dick to forgive, and I did. I'm trying to love, get married, and have me some wolf babies, shit.*" Mi *stood on business about her man, and I respected that. It was all that I could do.*

My arm went around her neck, and I pulled her to me. "*I love you, best friend.*" *We hugged each other tightly. Our asses were hanging off the seats. Before we knew it, we were on the floor with the giggles.* Yeah, we're more drunk than we planned to be.

WE'D BEEN AT THE LOUNGE SINCE SIX-THIRTY THAT *evening and it was after ten. It was time to go. There weren't a lot of people outside. "Bitch, let's sit in the car and I'll call Sabastian to come get us. I'on wanna just stand out here," Mi said with a pout.*

"Ma'am, if we were going to do that, we could have stayed in there," I fussed. I didn't want to sit in a damn car. "Why don't we leave the car here and rideshare to our place? He can pick us up from there."

Mi nodded, then said, "Okay, cool. You order the ride and I'll call Sabastian. Let me get my blanket out my car."

We started our trek to her car, arm in arm singing. Without warning, something knocked me on the back of my head. I fell over which pulled Mikayla down. Before we could react, various kicks and punches came to both of our bodies. "Yeah, bitch! You thought you was going to get away with how you handled a nigga," a deep voice roared. "Nah, bitch!"

Through the pain, I immediately recognized Parker's voice. A stomp on my leg caused me to scream in agonizing pain. "Stop, please stop!"

I reached for my best friend. My eyes opened quickly so see Mi on the ground passed out. They still assaulted her although she was helpless. A punch to my face involuntarily made my eyes close. My nose cracked loudly.

"Yeah, ho! I shoulda let my homeboys take that pussy!" A final kick to the face rendered me completely helpless.

The last thing that I heard was Parker telling someone 'good looking out'. When I heard Shakina's voice, I wanted to die. This bitch was really off her rocker. Next, I heard someone scream that they were calling the police before rushed footsteps came toward us and others fled. I willed myself to stay awake like the person who consoled me told me to, but it was no use. Blackness met me quickly.

Some Time Later...

"I'm good," a voice said. I wasn't sure whose voice it was because my eyes were closed. "Ma, I told you I don't need anything to eat."

My throat hurt. I tried to talk but was unable to. *What the hell!* All I could do was moan. The assumption that I was laying in a bed was substantiated when I felt the bed dip.

"Baby girl, Daddy is here. Get the doctor!" His voice was loud. "Baby, open your eyes for me. Your mama, Thaddeus, and Mrs. Parie are here too. Please open your eyes."

My father was not an overly emotional man. To hear the cries and desperation in his voice was enough motivation to try to open my eyes. After a few tries, I was able to successfully accomplish the task. My vision was blurry.

"Miss Sanders, can you hear me?" someone asked. "If you can hear me just nod your head. Take your time."

I softly gave him a nod. He told me that the nurse would take out my breathing tube. *Breathing tube?* I waited for the nurse while I looked around the room at all the worried expressions. My mother and father had wet faces. Thaddeus wore a heavy scowl with a mixture of concern. The tube being pulled out of my throat hurt.

When I coughed, it hurt. My bed was at a slight incline when my mother came over with a cup of water. "Here, baby. Try to drink this slowly." When the cup hit my bottom lip, I allowed the water to slowly go down my throat.

The water came out the side of my mouth. My father patted the sides of my mouth as the water came out.

Once I was done with the water, the doctor started to ask me questions about where I was, whether I knew who I was, and who the people in the room were. My voice was raspy, but I answered the best that I could. After checking my vitals, he checked my injuries while telling me what they were as he checked.

My heart broke as he listed my injuries. A broken nose, dislocated jaw, three broken ribs, and a broken leg and arm that I would need rehabilitation for. There was swelling of my brain which kept me in a medically induced coma for it to go down.

"Whe-where is Mikayla? Is she all right?" I asked barely over a whisper. I cared more about her than I did myself.

My mother stepped forward. "She's a few doors down, baby. She doing better."

When I told her I wanted to see her, the doctor responded. "We'll see what we can do. She's in pretty bad shape too."

"Sabastian is with her, Beauty." Thaddeus finally broke his silence. When our focus locked on each other, the hurt in his eyes swallowed me.

The doctor started to talk about the next steps and what I could expect in the coming weeks. I was not pleased that I'd have to be in the hospital longer, but I understood. "Who will you be staying with after you leave the hospital? You will need substantial assistance for a while."

Thaddeus stepped forward. "She's going to be staying at our home with me," he informed the doctor. "I've taken a leave of absence from my job to make sure that she's taken care of. Just let me know what she needs and if I need to make any modifications to my home."

"Yes, she will be staying with Thaddeus," my father confirmed. I guessed this was his way of giving me his approval of the plan. It wasn't needed because I wanted to be near him. I needed to be near him.

The doctor smiled. "That's great. I will make sure the physical therapist gets with you as well as the nurse for aftercare. We have some time for that."

After the doctor left my parents and Mrs. Parie messed over me before they stepped out to go get something to eat with Mrs. Parie. Thaddeus pulled the chair up next to my bed, then laid his head down on the bed. The sound of sniffling could be heard. My hand went to the back of his head.

"Beauty, I thought I was going to lose you. I've never been so scared in my life," he said with a pained voice. His head lifted, displaying his tears. "I should have been there. Fuck, this is my fault. I'm so sorry."

With my weak voice, I replied, "No, this is not on you. Mi and I should have never attacked him and Shakina. We should have left well enough alone."

"Don't do that, Elsbeth!" he griped. "That nigga deserved to get his ass beat." His brows dipped toward his nose. "That bitch boy and his friend conspired to rape you, Beauty. Do you hear me? Rape you. This is not your fault, and I wouldn't allow you to think it was."

What he said was true, but in my mind, it was cause and effect. They conspired to rape me. That resulted in me and Mi breaking into Shakina's house. We beat up her and Parker. Now we were here. I should have called the cops after the attempted rape, but what was I supposed to say to them? I didn't remember anything that I could tell the police. On top of that, Thaddeus and his friends or pack members shot some of them.

Thad stood, then leaned over me. His fingers stroked my face. "Give me a kiss."

"My breath stinks," I whined lowly. My breath had to have smelled like hot shit. Based on what the doctor said, I'd been in the coma for almost a damn month.

He scoffed. "You think I give a fuck about your stink breath? You're going to be my mate and wife." His face hovered over mine. "I'm getting my kiss."

His lips locked with mine. The relief and ease that came from the kiss and him being in my presence felt amazing. I missed him so much.

"Beauty." Thad's voice was soft. "I love you. Just to let you know as far as I'm concerned you are my mate already." He placed his lips near my ear. "I'm going to kill Parker, Shakina, and his friends in the most beastly way that I know how."

A chill ran down my spine. It wasn't because I didn't want him to do it. I knew if he didn't do it, my father would some way, somehow. The chill was accompanied with a sense of arousal at the fact that his man would go to these lengths to protect me. Was this love? If it was, I would want it all and forever.

A Little Time Later...

I didn't get to see Mikayla for almost a week and a half after I woke up in the hospital. I was so happy that Sabastian was there by her side with Sabian. Her injuries were not as severe as mine, but she did have a broken arm and two broken ribs. She left the hospital before I did. Like Thaddeus, Sabastian moved her into his house.

122

When the time came for me to leave the hospital, I was elated. My parents rode to Lumberton to help Thaddeus make sure that I was set up properly. Thaddeus insisted that my parents stay for as long as they felt comfortable. They took him up on his offer and stayed a week.

During that week, my mama and Mrs. Parie got close. Every day, my mama, Mrs. Parie, or Rummie cooked breakfast, lunch, and dinner. I was surprised that Thad's dad didn't come by to meet my father. When I asked about him Rummie, Thad, and Mrs. Parie were vague. They told me that he was away on business. I knew that was a lie because I'd seen him knocking on the door of his house. Why a man would knock on his own door baffled me.

"Baby, stop playing with me," Thad said in a grumpy tone. It was two o'clock in the morning and I was horny. We were lying in the bed, and I was trying to get some dick unapologetically.

My hand massaged his dick slowly. "Baby, it's been forever since I had some dick. I want some." I was begging unashamedly. I felt like a crackhead or dickhead, however you wanted to see it.

Thad rolled on his side to face me. My baby was tired, and I felt kind of bad, but I needed him. "Beauty, your leg is not one hundred percent, and I am not about to fuck up your progress. You want me to eat your flower?"

Thad ate pussy like he lived in a concentration camp, and it was the only nourishment he would ever receive. "Thad, I appreciate every lick, suck, and slither of your tongue, however, I want some wolf dick." This was the first time that I referenced him as a wolf. *My desperation is showing.*

His eyebrow tip toed toward his hairline. "Let me get this straight, Elsbeth Darya Sanders. The first time you acknowledge me as a wolf is when you request some of my wolf dick." He chortled. "Beauty, go to sleep. You got me fucked up. You in here talking about wolf dick, but you haven't sat down to have an adult conversation about me being a wolf."

"Thaddeus, that's not fair. Me being here tells you that I've accepted that you're a wolf," I whined. All of this took away from the focus of me getting dick. He should have known that I accepted him fully.

"You being here doesn't tell me that. It tells me that you needed assistance." His face tightened. "I'm not those little boys that you're used to. I need you to communicate with me."

I'd be lying if I said his words didn't hurt my feelings. I understood what he said. I even agreed, but that didn't mean that I wanted to hear the shit. "Okay, I'm sorry. I should have said and made sure you understood that I accept all of you for you." I took a deep breath, then said, "I love you, Thaddeus." This was the first time that I'd said it since he confessed his love to me.

He stared at me for a moment before he kissed my lips. "I love you, Elsbeth. I'm happy that you accept me and my beast." He kissed my lips again. "You're still not getting this wolf dick right now."

What in the no dick hell is this? "Thad, baby, what if I lay on my side and you just stick it in from the back and stroke me ever so lightly?" I displayed my biggest pout. "You can even tip me out."

His face contorted. "What the hell does it mean to tip you out, Beauty?" He was already laughing.

"You can just stroke me with the tip from the back. I'll lay on my side," I explained. "I miss you."

He shook his head with a smirk. "Come here, crazy ass

girl." He pulled me into him, then kissed my lips passion-ately. "I love your silly ass."

His hand gripped my ass. Excitement took over me as his lips moved to my neck and one hand left my ass cheek to my breast. Since I'd been here, I made sure I slept with the least amount of clothes on. Just in case he ever wanted to play, stick, or lick my body flower he would have easy access.

"Turn over," he instructed with his deep voice that I loved. He didn't have to tell me twice. His hand went to my waist to help me.

Once I was on my side with my back to his front, he growled into my ear. It was more animalistic than I'd ever heard. "Elsbeth, you want to be my mate?" His question penetrated my soul. He slowly filled my body flower. I guess he said fuck that tip shit.

"Yes!" My answer came out louder than I intended it to be. He asked me again, and with no hesitation I restated my answer. "Yes, yes! I'll be your mate, slut, wife, wolfette, or whatever."

His strokes slowed until they halted. "Wolfette? Really, Beauty?"

"I'm just saying. I love you. I want you and your beast." I reached my hand behind myself to touch his abs. When my hand got to its destination, I tapped them. "Let's go. Fuck me!"

He wrapped his hand around my neck, then pulled me back. "I got you. Let's be clear from this moment on you are my mate. Be prepared for my ma and sister to prepare you for a mating ceremony."

I heard his words. Whether I fully understood them was up for debate because his dick was stroking me to the most euphoric place that I'd ever had the pleasure of visiting. Ceremony and Ma was all I heard for sure, but that didn't stop me from agreeing.

Our sex from the side/back lasted way longer than I thought it would, broken leg and all. The entire time he dicked me down, he made sure my broken leg was comfortable. By the time we finished, I was ready to go into the sleep that his transcended sexual skill triggered. He took care of cleaning us up while I lay in the bed.

"Get some rest, Beauty. You got some long days ahead of you," Thaddeus said before he kissed my neck, then wrapped his arm around me. We both fell into a comfortable silence, then slumber.

A Few Nights Later...

"Kayla, can I have some ice cream?" Sabian asked my best friend with the cutest pout. He was the cutest little boy, I swear.

Me, Mikayla, Jorie, Rummie, Farad, Thad, and Sabastian were at Thad's house having a little game night. Sabian originally was going to spend time with Mama Parie, as she told me to call her now, but Mi told her that she wanted him with her. The relationship that my best friend and Sabastian's son had developed was heartwarming. When Thad told me the story of how Sabian's mother just left him, I was ready to find her and beat her ass. It was a shame that she was willing to miss out on an amazing child.

Sabian was sitting next to Mikayla on the couch cuddled to her side. Before she could tell him yes like I knew she would, Sabastian spoke up. "Sabian, no. You're not about to be bouncing off the wall all night."

Sabian's face fell with disappointment. Sabastian was sitting on the left side of Mi and Sabian on the right. Mi's neck snapped in Sabastian's direction. "Baby, why not? I'll stay up with him," she whined.

All the men snickered. Her evil eye hit all of them. "Baby, I love you, but you know good and well your ass is going to fall asleep as soon as your lids get heavy. You're going to be sleeping and that damn boy is going to be jumping on my damn head trying to knock the Mario coins out of it."

Mi didn't like to hear that, but Sabastian told all of the truth. My best friend was not one that could stay awake past a certain time. She had literally fallen asleep in the club before. Mi leaned close to Sabian, then poorly whispered in his ear. "When Daddy goes to sleep, we'll have an ice cream party, just me and you."

Thaddeus guffawed. "That shit better happen at your house." I elbowed him from my seat between his legs. "What! I'm just saying, baby."

We sat on the lounger across from the couch. Rummie was in the kitchen caking on the phone. She tried to be discrete, but the girls caught on very fast. When she came in the den where we were and told us that she was making a run, I knew what it was. The urgency in her voice told me that she was about to run to a dick. The girls needed a night to catch up.

We all decided to watch a movie together. We were fifteen minutes into the movie when Sabian blurted, "Daddy, you look tired. You should go to sleep." He got out of his seat, stepped in front of his father, then held his hand out to him. "Come on, Daddy. I'll tuck you in."

Farad erupted into laughter from the other side of the

sectional couch. He was cuddled up with Jorie. "That boy wants that ice cream party bad."

Sabastian's phone rang as he glared at his son with a smile. "You lucky this phone ringing, son." He scooped Sabian into his arms. "If not, we'd have to have a tickle fight." Sabastian tickled him for a few seconds before putting him down and answering his phone. He listened silently for a moment before he left the room. He told Farad and Thaddeus to follow him.

"I'm mad you got that lil boy trying to put his daddy in bed," Jorie said with giggles. Jorie lived in Raleigh too, but since her and Farad became official, she considered moving back. Her and Farad were so cute together.

Naturally, Mikayla and I had to take a leave of absence from work. Our school was gracious enough to allow us to finish out the year through virtual classes. We were both grateful since we were so close to graduating. Sabian cuddled back in his original spot at Mi's side. He talked about his dad looking tired, but he looked like he was about to pass out himself.

Several minutes after the guys went to the back, they came back out. Their facial expressions were not of the joyous variety. Sabastian and Farad didn't sit back in their original seats. Thaddeus came over and took a seat in front of me on the lounger. "Baby, you remember that thing we talked about in the hospital?"

I didn't have to wrack my brain to know what he was referring to. We'd had multiple conversations about the situation with Parker. "Yes, baby, I remember."

"Well, we're about to handle that," he confirmed. "I told you that I would never leave you out of the loop if I didn't have to." After I nodded acknowledgement to his statement, he leaned forward and kissed my lips. "All of you stay here until we get back," he instructed all of the women.

Jorie waved him off. "We're not going anywhere. We got a mating ceremony to plan."

Farad and Sabastian kissed their women, and Thad gave me another kiss before they left. I noticed when Thaddeus came from the back, he was dressed in all black. That was not what he had on when they went to the back.

The second they left, Jorie started in on the mating ceremony. There hadn't been much conversation about this ceremony, so I had a lot of questions. Jorie explained the importance of the mating ceremony which I now understood was a different event from the wedding. The mating ceremony was only for pack and tribe members. That scared me because I wanted my best friend to be there. Jorie made a joke about Mikayla and I going through our mating ceremony together. I believed that wholeheartedly.

Sabian didn't last an hour into our conversation before Mikayla took him to the spare bedroom to lie down. The doorbell stopped our conversation. I glanced down at my watch, wondering who could be at the door after midnight. Thaddeus added me to his home security account; therefore, I had access to his cameras and door locks. After I grabbed my phone to see who it was, I smiled. "Oh, it's Mr. Lourie." I told him to come in, then unlocked the lock from the app on my phone.

He hadn't been over since I'd been here. When he walked into the den where we were, I noticed the grimace that sat on his face. "Hey, Mr. Lourie. I haven't seen you since I've been here. You're right on time because we were talking about the mating ceremony."

Jorie said that the chief was the person that performed the ceremony. I wanted to ask him some questions as well.

He stopped and glared back at Jorie who returned his glare after he moved and stood near the fireplace. I was confused with the tension that suddenly filled the room. I'm not naive enough to say that I thought he was my biggest fan, but I also didn't think he had an issue with me.

"Elsbeth and Mikayla, I would say that it's nice to see you, but that would be a lie," he spat with no real emotion. *What the hell!* "As far as the mating ceremony, there will not be one."

Mikayla shifted in her seat, then said, "Hold the hell on. Who pissed in your succotash?" She pointed at herself, me, then Jorie. "None of us did it to you."

I was too shocked by his demeanor to say anything. He was hella disrespectful, but I didn't want to reciprocate the disrespect just yet because he was still Thaddeus's father. Now, all of the vagueness around the question of where he was started to make sense to me. The man clearly didn't like me or Mikayla.

He scoffed lowly. "On top of my son and Sabastian falling in love with beastless women, they fell in love with disrespectful ones." He spoke to himself more than he did to us. His eyes zeroed on me. "I want to make this clear. My son will not mate, marry, or be with you. You are not worthy of being with a beast man."

Jorie stood to her feet. "Chief Pat, you are doing way too much right now. This is the woman that your son has chosen. This is who he will mate and marry."

"A whore finally cons someone into potentially mating her and she becomes mouthy," Chief Pat snapped at Jorie. "Sit down and stay in your place. You are just as worthless as these two beastless women."

The hurt covered Jorie's expression while shock covered mine and Mikayla's. I didn't know much about

Jorie's past, but I knew she had one like we all did. She'd lived on the reservation all of her life. Her parents still lived here, but they were estranged. She sat down, but something told me that she was telepathically calling for rein-forcement.

"Mr. Lourie, I'm not sure why you're here or what brought this on, but I love Thaddeus," I professed. "I will be with him. We will get mated and married and we will have children."

When Mr. Lourie stepped toward me, Jorie stood with a growl. He simply scoffed with a chuckle, but his steps stopped. "Elsbeth, the day you mate my son is the last day that you'll be on this earth."

Mikayla jumped up as quickly as she could with a broken arm. Jorie jumped in front of her. "Bitch, you got us fucked up. I don't give a fuck what wolf you got!"

"Patrick!" What sounded like Mama Parie's voice came booming through Thad's house. Like a bat out of hell she came into the den. "What did I tell you about fucking with my babies?"

His lips tightened as his chest rose and fell rapidly. "Parie, the only children we have are Thaddeus and Rumble. None of these bitch—"

"I don't give a fuck about any of that, Patrick! So we have a clear understanding... Thaddeus, Rumble, Elsbeth, Mikayla, Farad, Sabastian, and Jorie are my babies. Fuck with any one of them and you'll have to see me." Mama Parie stepped into Mr. Lourie's face. "Get the fuck out of my son's house, now."

They had a stare-off with one another. It felt like all the oxygen was taken out of the room while they stood there. His head dropped slightly with a shake. With a tight jaw, he said, "I'll see you, my love."

"Bye, bitch. Tell Chepi I said she needs to keep you busy," she said with a titter. "You're doing way too much."

He strolled out of the house like he was supposed to be here. I was still seated on the couch with no understanding of what just happened or why. Mama Parie took the seat next to me, wrapped her arm around me, then gently pulled my body into hers. "I'm so sorry, baby."

Mikayla was fuming with tears running down her cheeks. She told us that she was going to check on Sabian. When she left the room, I turned to Mama Parie. "What did I do wrong?"

Thaddeus

Now that I had Beauty in my house, she was never leaving. Furthermore, my baby didn't want to leave. While she was in the hospital, I had a talk with her father first to let him know that I was going to take care of her. It was a fruitful conversation that allowed me to express my love and clear intention for his daughter. After a deep dive interrogation, he accepted the love that I expressed for his daughter. Regardless of his deep dive, there was no mention from me of my wolf origin. That was not information that he needed at this time.

Beauty was worried about not being able to finish school. Graduation was right around the corner. Both her and Mikayla had worked hard. When the ladies found out that they could complete their classes to satisfy their graduation requirements virtually, it was a major stress relief. When Beauty wasn't resting, relaxing, or asking me to fuck her, she was doing schoolwork.

"Yeah, that's his lil trap house if that's what you want to call it," Oscar said from the driver's seat of the SUV we were in. "From what I saw earlier, there are five dudes and two females inside. I haven't seen anyone leave or come."

When Oscar heard about the attack, he took that shit personally. From that day, he got a team together to start looking for this Parker bitch and his bitch boys. The team found out that Parker's main residence was in Charlotte with his girlfriend. That's where he fled to after the attack in an attempt to evade possible arrest. The police were the last of his worries. The girls told the police they had no idea who attacked them.

"Let me check it out," I said before I climbed out of the SUV. If this was a trap house it was poorly secured. I wasn't going to act like I ever sold drugs or any shit like that, but I knew no one should be able to just walk up on a trap house. "These niggas are dumb," I mumbled under my breath.

I stepped on the lawn in front of the shabby house. Adjusting my eyes, they x-rayed through the wall. Oh, they were having a whole little party with that Shakina bitch and her friend as entertainment. There were four guys sitting on the couch with the two girls dancing in front of them with little clothes on. The music could be heard from where I stood in the lawn. A presence stood next to me. Without looking, I knew it was Farad.

"Let's see what these fuckas are talking about," Farad said. His sonar gift was one of the coolest gifts that I'd ever seen in a wolf. He told me that his gift was like having high tech earbuds in his ears all the time. It allowed him to amplify sound, cancel sound, and isolate sound.

While I stood there to see, he stood next to me to listen. We were silent for a moment. "Man, they not talking about much of shit. The girls are about to get run through, that's about it," Farad said. He pivoted his body to face me. "How you wanna do this?"

"Let's get back in the truck and discuss the plan." We both walked back to the SUV and got into it. The fact that there were two blacked out SUVs in front of the house where these dudes were, and they were none the wiser baffled me. How do you call yourself a drug dealer but aren't vigilant about knowing what's going on around you at all times? Each SUV had four men in it from my pack. That was more men than I needed since we were all wolves.

We discussed the plan telepathically for the most part so the others in the SUV behind us would be included. The final decision was to go in like normal human beings with our toolies. For the actual demise, only me, Sabastian, and Oscar planned to shift. We checked our weapons to make sure we were ready to go before we moved forward with our plan.

We all moved stealthily toward the house. All the individuals in the house were in the same places they were in before Farad and I walked back to the SUV. With one kick to the flimsy front door, it came off the hinges. When we came up with this plan, my mind told me that these bums would be armed and dangerous. All of their guns were on a table that wasn't close enough for them to reach it quickly to defend themselves. They were outgunned and outnumbered. We were on their ass.

The butt of my gun went to Shakina's head. "Bitch, shut the fuck up! Your ass wasn't screaming when you set my girl up to one: be raped, then two: be jumped." I hit her again. "Shut the fuck up!"

On any normal day, I would never assault a woman. This was not a normal day, and this was not a woman. You fuck with the beast or anything the beast loves; you get the teeth.

"Please don't hurt us! I apologized to her. She didn't

care," Shakina cried. She and her friend who I recognized from the hotel room with the initial incident occurred, cowered against the wall.

Farad came over to watch them so that I could address this bitch Parker. This ho ass fucka was sitting on the couch with a gun at his head, a frown on his face, and a tear on his cheek. "What's the tear for, young man? Are you feeling remorseful yet since you're about to lose your life for fucking with my woman?"

"Your woman? Man, I don't even know you. Who is your woman?" Parker feigned ignorance like a dummy.

Oscar, who held the gun to his head, guffawed. "Boy, you've got to be fucking delusional if you don't remember the niggas that ran up in a hotel room where you and ya fuck boys were going to rape a female." He leaned over to look at the other three dudes that sat there terrified. One of them had pissed his pants. "These the two that got those bullets to the hand."

"Parker, because I don't have the time to go back and forth with you, I'm going to make this simple. We are here today because you and this bitch back here..." I pointed to Shakina who was cried and sat in a pool of piss against the wall. "Y'all decided to attempt to rape, then jumped my girl and my bro Sabastian's girl." I tilted my head toward Sabastian so they would know who he was.

I stepped closer to the couch. "We're not going to go through the whys of what you did because it would prolong the inevitable. I'm ready to get home to my mate." I tilted my head. "You fucked up severely, my boy. You should be mindful of who you fuck with because you never know who that person is connected to."

"Man, I'm sorry." Parker allowed the tears to freely flow down his face. "I was mad about how her and her homegirl did me and Shakina. Elsbeth didn't get raped, so she should have left well enough alone."

Did this bitch say that my woman should have left well enough alone? There was no way that he said that shit out loud. My fangs grew and I exposed them.

The four men pushed back on the couch as if they had anywhere to go. "What the fuck!" one of them yelled. "What the fuck are you?"

One of my pack members switched places with Oscar and another switched places with Farad. Mine, Farad, and Oscar's guns were handed over so that we could progress to the next part of the night.

"What the fuck I am, is a beast." I shifted into my beast, then immediately pounced onto Parker. My teeth latched onto his neck and pulled his pharynx right out with ease. I didn't need to do all of the extra shit.

The screams in the living room were loud. I saw Sabastian shift from the corner of my eye as I stalked toward Shakina. More screams and a deep growl came from behind me. I knew Sabastian was handling his business. My head turned toward Oscar to give him the signal to shift himself. Shakina's flight response took over and she tried to bolt toward the door. *Silly ass dummy.*

I lunged the short distance to wrap my mouth around her leg to bring her down. The agony of her screams warmed my heart. Although I would love to relish in the moment, I needed her to shut the fuck up. Since she wanted to run behind her fuck buddy Parker, it would be cute if they had matching wounds. Her pharynx would look adorable next to his. Once I had it out of her neck, I placed it on the floor right next to her fuck buddy's.

Once we knew that all bodies had moved on to the afterlife, one of our pack members went to the truck to get us clothing to shift back. After we were back in human form, dressed in our tees and basketball shorts, and grabbed everything that we came with, we left. The door was left open because I didn't give a fuck. *Fuck them!*

It was after three in the morning. We all were ready to get to my house to be with our mates. Farad told us earlier in the night that he planned to ask Jorie to be his mate. We were going to see if the ladies wanted to do a joint mating ceremony. Those ceremonies and celebrations were not cheap. On top of that, we needed to find someone to do the ceremony. I had an idea, but first we needed to solidify a date.

"Let's get home to our mates, fellas. I miss my woman," I commented. Like thieves in the night, we were on our way back to Lumberton. I needed a shower, my woman, and a bed.

THE HEAVINESS WAS FELT THE SECOND THAT I STEPPED into my house. Something wasn't right. My mother met us before we could walk out of the foyer. "Y'all go take a shower. Before you go to your mates and wake them up, come speak with me in the den." She grabbed the big black trash bag that Farad had in his hand. "I will burn these while you all shower."

I didn't like it! What the fuck happened that she didn't want us to speak with our mates first? She let us know that Mikayla was in the guest room with Sabian and Jorie was in the other guest room while Elsbeth was in our room. "All right, Ma. It shouldn't take us too long."

Before we walked out, she asked us if everything was clean and clear with what we had to do tonight. We assured her that it was. Each of us went our separate ways to take our showers.

When I entered my bedroom, Beauty was asleep in the bed. I went over to check on her. I pulled the covers back slowly to check her body. I'm not sure why the fear that someone attacked her overtook me, but it did. She shifted in her sleep but didn't wake up. After I kissed her forehead, I went to the bathroom to take care of my hygiene. My mind traveled to the different scenarios of what my mother might tell me when we got back to the den.

I was the last one to get to the den. Farad and Sabastian were eating. We had an additional guest now. "Rummie, what you doing here? You ran out of here earlier like you had hot coals in ya ass. What's the coals name?"

She rolled her eyes before she told me to mind my business. I would for now, but we would revisit this at a later time and date. She'd been sneaking around for a little time now. I knew it had to do with a man but wasn't sure if it was a human or beast. I assumed if it was a beast we would know, but my assumption could be completely wrong.

"Here, baby boy, eat something." She handed me a nice plate of food that she cooked. I was confused why she came over here and cooked in the wee hours of the morning when Rummie cooked earlier in the night. Everything on the plate were foods that were my favorite. *Yeah, this is about to be some bullshit.*

"Ma, what's going on? I want to go lay up under my mate," I said after I swallowed my first bite of food. *Damn this food is good.*

My mother sat on the couch next to Rummie, who clearly knew what the hell was going on. When she started to talk, we listened silently. Midway through her telling us about what transpired earlier, we had all put our plates down. My anger was building by the second. All I could see in the moment was red and death. After what happened earlier tonight, I had a certain amount of blood thirst that I still craved.

"Just so we're clear, your husband threatened to kill my mate?" I wanted to make sure that I didn't misconstrue anything that was told to us. It would be a shame to kill my father because of a misunderstanding.

My mother dropped her head. When she lifted it, tears laced her lids. "Son, I am so sorry that your father is doing this. I don't know what has gotten into him," she cried. "For as long as I've known him, he had whined about this pure bloodline that I never understood. He's not pureblood, clearly. Look at you both! The Louries bloodline had never been pure. Those niggas loved black pussy!"

The gasp that left Rummie's mouth was hilarious. "Mama! Why would you say that?"

"Girl, shut up! I may be one hundred percent Siouan blood, but it is clear your daddy is not, that's one. Also, tell me what Chepi is?" my mother asked.

Ah shit! Chepi was in fact a black woman that was the stepdaughter of one of our tribe members after her black mother married him. She was one when her mom married. They legally changed her name to Chepi once it was all said and done with. "She's a black woman," Rummie confirmed.

"Exactly," my mother said with a side-eye. "Your father has always hated his darker skin and oh, he hated when you two were born and y'all shared it. It was even a hue darker than his." She shook her head and looked up to the ceiling like she had just recalled a memory. "I remember overhearing him tell an elder that he felt cursed because of his ancestors mixing the blood. His dark skin had been passed down to his children." She pointed at me. "Here you come,

Thaddeus, with a black beauty to further water down the bloodline in his eyes."

Sabastian chuckled, then said, "With all due respect, Mama Parie. That's y'all family issues. Patrick talking shit to my mate will be dealt with in whatever manner I see fit."

Farad agreed with Sabastian before I spoke up. "Yeah, I think I'll pay him a visit once the sun rises. I'll allow him a peaceful night with his whore."

Without another word, I stood, kissed my mother and sister, told my bros goodnight and went to lay with Beauty. Once I was in the room, I climbed in the bed. She instantaneously wrapped her body around mine as best as she could, considering her broken leg and arm. I kissed her forehead. "I love you, Elsbeth."

She moaned, tightened her one arm around me, then said, "I love you too, baby. Please don't ever leave me." Her head tilted back. I could see her face from the illumination that was given off from the television that was still on. The sadness in her eyes bothered the fuck out of me. There was insecurity there and that was not all right.

I leaned my head down to kiss her lips. After I did, I said, "I'm not going anywhere, and neither are you. You got a wolf behind you now, for life."

She gave me a small smile before she laid her head back on my chest. Soon after, I heard her soft snores. My father would have to answer for his blatant and unforgiveable disrespect. I didn't give a fuck about his self-hatred about his lineage. We fucking black and Indian. It was what it was.

Later the Same Morning...

The sun hadn't been up for an hour before me, Farad, and Sabastian were on our way to Chepi's house. When we pulled up to her house, I huffed when I saw my mother's car parked on the curb. She got out of her car after we parked. I became more annoyed when my sister diddy-bopped out of the passenger side of the car.

Ma came to my driver's side window, then knocked. I rolled the window down with a smile. "Yes, Ma. Why are you here?"

"I'm here because I'm the mama wolf. I'm here to make sure my baby wolves are all right," she said with a stern tone. What my mother said went. There was no way that I was going to tell her that she should leave. No matter how old I am, I'm still her child. Parie Lourie had no problem reminding me of that fact.

I nodded, then said, "All right, Ma. Let's get this over with." I climbed out of my car after my mother stepped back. Farad and Sabastian stepped out of the car as well.

When we got onto the front porch, my mother stopped me. "Let me knock on the door, son." I let her have her way. It's not like I had another option. She knocked on the door all sweetly and shit like we were here to sell World's Finest Chocolate or some shit.

A minute later, Chepi answered. "Parie, what are you doing here?" The shock that sat on her face was laughable. Side hos always want to be surprised when their shit comes home to roost.

"Good morning, Chepi. I'm here to see Patrick. May we come in?" Ma's voice was sweetly menacing.

Chepi looked behind herself nervously. We knew my

father was there because his truck was in the driveway. "Um, Parie, I'm about to cook—"

My mother pushed the half-opened door back. "Bitch, I don't have time for this bullshit. Let me in this fucking house."

Chepi's body went into the wall. She grabbed my mother's arm, but quickly pulled her hand back when my mother's fangs exposed themselves. Chepi didn't have a beast, so she was careful when it came to those who did.

We all walked into the house like we paid the mortgage. Me, my mother, and sister had been inside Chepi's house hundreds of times. My mother told us to go sit in the den before she headed up the stairs. Chepi came into the den with an attitude. "Are you going to cook breakfast or nah, God Mama Ho?" Rummie rudely asked. "You know I love your strawberry pancakes."

"Really, Sis!" I burst into laughter. "How you gonna call that lady a ho, then ask her for some strawberry pancakes? She's going to poison your ass."

Rummie kissed her teeth. "Chepi doesn't want to be wolf food. She knows better."

Seconds later, footsteps were heard coming down the stairs. "What the fuck are y'all doing here? You have no right to be here!"

My feet moved to where my father stood at the bottom of the stairs. After I stepped into his face, I reintroduced his face to my fist. He fell back on the stairs. "And you had the right to come into my home and threaten my mate?"

Chepi rushed to my father. In the process, she pushed me back. "Have you lost your damn mind!"

My mother grabbed her by her hair and pulled her back. "Don't put your hands on my fucking son." One thing about wolves, our strength was not matched to humans. My mother's action caused Chepi to fly back more than anticipated.

My father got himself together and stood. "You disrespectful nigger. After all that I've done for you."

My mother looked at Chepi. "Is this the man you love?" she asked. "This man sleeps in your black ass bed that's in your black ass house and dives into your black ass pussy but can stand here and call his son that came from him a nigger."

Chepi looked bothered but she refrained from saying anything. I felt an ounce of pity for my father, but not enough to stop my fist from colliding with his face again. "What have you done for me? You disrespected all of our mates." I pointed between Farad and Sabastian.

My father was still laid back on the stairs. I hovered over him. "I don't have all day to go back and forth with a self-hating bitch. I will marry Elsbeth, and I will mate her. You have no control over it no matter what you think. If you ever in your miserable life threaten my mate, I will kill you."

"You would kill me over that black bitch?" The venom in my father's voice was strong. "That bitch means more to you than the pack. Is that what you're telling me?"

Sabastian stepped forward. "Your actions are not aligned to the pack or in the best interest of the pack. Chief or not, you don't speak for the pack."

My mother stepped to my father's side, then glared down at him. "I told you before to stop fucking with my babies. You're running out of chances." She glanced at Chepi. "I want you to pay close attention to how the love of your life speaks. You wonder why he's never tried to leave me to be with you?" She stepped closer to Chepi who had yet to get her ass up from the floor.

"If he hates his own skin, what makes you think that he

could love you or yours? Yeah, he may love that pussy, but that was always it," my mother said. She leaned down over Chepi who shook. "Make your next move the best move for yourself and your safety." She looked at all of us. "We are done here. Let's go. I have a mating ceremony to plan."

We all started to walk toward the door. My father couldn't leave well enough alone and had to have the last word. "How are you going to have a mating ceremony without me?"

With a wide smile, I looked over my shoulder. "You're not the only Lourie we know that has the rank to perform the ceremony. You're not invited by the way."

Elsbeth

Mating Ceremony...

My stomach was doing flips. Today was the day of me, Mikayla, and Jorie's mating ceremony. We decided to have a joint ceremony so that we could experience it together as friends. The ceremony felt like it creeped up on us. When the date was planned, I breathed a sigh of relief knowing it was months away. Those months slapped me in the face early this morning like *hey bitch*.

"You are so beautiful." Mama Parie came over and stood next to me. "My baby boy might cry today," she teased. She played with the ceremonial attire that I wore.

Rummie giggled. "Oh, he's going to cry for sure. He's lucky we can't have cameras out during the ceremony." Rummie and Thaddeus's relationship was funny to me. It made me wish I had a sibling.

I smiled, then responded, "Thank you, Mama Parie." I gave her a shaky smile.

Obviously, my parents couldn't participate or attend the

ceremony. They didn't even know about it, but that didn't make me feel bad. My mother was so engulfed with planning our wedding which was three months away.

Mama Parie moved around the room to check on Mikayla and Jorie. Jorie's mother was here with her, which I knew made her happy. Jorie and her parents reconciled months ago when they heard that she was to be mated. The women in the tribe fawned over us.

The past months had been interesting to say the least. Thaddeus's father had been quiet and not around. After the incident at his house that I was made privy to after the fact, Chepi decided it was in her best interest that she and Mr. Lourie not be involved. She kicked him out and he's been staying at his cousin's house. I was at Mama Parie's house when Chepi came over to apologize.

I really thought they were going to reconcile. While Chepi poured her heart and tears out in the apology, Mama Parie started crying. She listened as Chepi talked and held her hand. Hell, I sat there at the kitchen nook crying myself. After Chepi was finished, Mama Parie stood and circled the kitchen island where they had the conversation. She invited Chepi into a hug that she accepted.

When Mama Parie pulled back from the hug, she told Chepi to suck on a sick Indian dick and to stay the fuck away from her. You could have stuck a dick in my mouth at that moment because of how wide my mouth hung open. Mama Parie's voice was so soft and sincere. Chepi was just as shocked as I was. Long situation short, last month she moved off the reservation and hasn't been back since.

"Ladies, we have visitors." Mama Parie's voice sounded. Her smile was bright as she stood toward the front of the room that we got ready in. Her ceremonial garments were beautiful as well as all of the other women in the tribe.

There was a group of women standing next to her that I'd never seen before. I'd met pretty much everyone in the tribe since I'd been on the reservation. Mikayla and I permanently moved into our mates' homes a week after we agreed on the ceremony date. The tribe gave us a graduation party when we graduated a few months ago. We were now in talks about the pharmacy that would be opened on the reservation.

"Ladies, I wanted to introduce you all to some Lourie family that originated right here on this reservation, but now live in Washington State," Mama Parie announced after she walked further into the room. She took the time to introduce us to the mates of the Lourie men that came down.

Visiting us from Washington State were Claire, Eyota, Sasha, Willow, Rebel, and Daanis. All of the women were married to Lourie men, except Willow who was a Lourie and Daanis who was married to the Chief of the Quileute tribe that they were a part of. They were all so beautiful and nice.

"Claire's husband, Mason Lourie Sr., will officiate the mating ceremony," Mama Parie informed us. She explained that Mason Sr. was a cousin that was born and raised on this reservation. Mason Sr. and his brother Kyle who was also here were elders in their tribe in Washington State. Kyle Jr., Kyle's son also came as well as their chief Arrow.

Mikayla, Jorie, and I rushed to greet and thank them for being here. We tried to offer handshakes, but they wouldn't accept them. We were pulled into hugs that were loving and genuine.

"You ladies are so beautiful," Claire said. She chuckled, then said, "Y'all also look nervous as hell." All of the women laughed.

Mikayla was the first of us to speak. "I'm very nervous and terrified." When Willow asked why she was terrified, my best friend admitted an insecurity that she hadn't even admitted to me. "Will I be enough for Sabastian? The tribe is amazing and learning about the wolf's origin is one of the most fascinating things that I'd ever seen. The fact is, I don't have a beast. I'm just a human with no beast or gifts."

My heart stopped because it was like I shared a heart with my best friend. My hand moved to hers, then gripped it. "I understand that feeling," I said with a sigh. "I think I feel the same way, especially knowing that Thaddeus's father doesn't want us together and Enola is still acting like a bitter baby's mother."

Daanis stepped forward. "First, fuck that Enola girl. We met her last night when we were introduced to her father, Ahote. She embarrassed the hell out of her father talking out of the side of her neck about the mixed blood shit." She shook her head.

Mama Parie sighed. "Clearly, she's not invited to this ceremony. I've known that little girl since she was born. She was the sweetest little thing. Honey, that child went to college and lost her coochie." She chuckled. "Ahote once had the same mindset of wanting a pure bloodline.

"I guess he changed that quickly after the council voted him out," Mama Parie disclosed. "Ahote isn't an idiot. He knows when to disconnect from a toxic cancer to save himself."

Mr. Patrick being voted out was new information to me. "Wait, he's not the chief of the tribe? What does that mean for the tribe?" I asked with curiosity. The tribe and pack culture were new for me and Mikayla. I loved that members were open to answering any questions that we had.

Rummie smiled, then said, "It means that your future

mate has the option to be the chief if that's what he wants per the counsel." She bumped my shoulder with hers. "Girl, you about to be the first lady of the tribe. Sis, you don't need to be a beast to be the shit."

"Ain't that the truth," Sasha said. "I didn't get my beast until after I had my son Tre. Imagine not having a beast then one day shifting into a centauride?"

Mikayla tilted her head. "Wait, what is a centauride?" she asked. "Is that like a breed of wolf?"

"Um, I have a different question. How can you shift into a beast when you don't have one?" I didn't miss her saying that shit. What was that about?

All the ladies looked at each other, then snickered. "We have so much to teach you ladies," Sasha responded before she wrapped her arm around my neck. "Let's get you ladies mated and officially a part of the tribe."

MIKAYLA, JORIE, AND I HAD REHEARSED THE MATING ceremony many times, but nothing could have prepared us for the intensity, beauty, and emotion that surrounded the ceremony. As his mother and sister thought, Thaddeus did indeed cry as I walked toward him. The women in the tribe danced before us as we made our way to the front altar. Thaddeus stood there in his tribal attire looking. After I saw the other Lourie men, it became abundantly clear that they all had fine in their bloodline.

Yes, Mr. Lourie was an asshole, but there was nothing unattractive about him. Mama Parie also was correct when she said that the Lourie men loved black pussy. It was interesting to hear the snippet of Claire's family's history. They were going to be here for a week, so there would be time to dig into it as well as the whole centauride thing.

Mikayla, Jorie, and I all made it to the front to stand in front of our respective mates. Thaddeus stared at me with wet cheeks. He stepped into my space, kissed my lips, then said, "You are beautiful and mine."

"All right, youngin," Mason Jr. said with laughter in his voice. "Let's get you through this ceremony and y'all can get on with that nasty Lourie shit we do."

The audience laughed at our expense. I didn't mind because I was in awe of everything that was going on around me. Everyone and thing were absolutely beautiful.

Mason Jr. looked between all the mating couples. "The moon shines above us as a reminder of the light in the darkness that we each can be. The darkness is a reminder of the beast that lies within. May the gods allow the light to lead us to the rivers of peace and tranquility. Mikayla and Elsbeth, I want you to know that the beast within you exists in the intensity of your love for your mate. Understand that you don't need a physical beast to have a gift. Love is enough of a beast to satisfy a beast."

His words brought me more peace and confidence than what he would ever know. He continued with the ceremony, and it was all transcending. Just as we got to the bonding portion of the ceremony, Mason Jr. stopped. An eerie expression took over his face. Suddenly, Thaddeus stepped back. I peeked over my shoulder toward Mikayla who wore a puzzled look.

There was a shift in the atmosphere that I couldn't explain. *Did I do something wrong?* My mind began to race about what could be wrong. Seconds later, Thaddeus yelled, "Get them out of here!"

Without warning, I was pulled back but not before a

wolf jumped toward me. I let out a loud scream from the sight of the beast and the force of me being pulled back. All around me, members of the pack shifted into their beasts. Mason and his crew turned into beasts as well, but all of them were not wolves. I had no idea what was happening.

While Mikayla and I were being pulled back, I noticed the wolf that lunged at me was fighting with a gray wolf. The gray wolf was winning. So much was going on that my mind couldn't comprehend what my eyes saw. After we were pulled inside of the building that we dressed in, I noticed that it was Rummie, Claire, and Jorie who had pulled us in.

"What's happening? Who was that?" I was in a panic. My ceremony was ruined. I rushed over to my best friend who was sitting on a couch crying. "Are you hurt?"

Mikayla's eyes bulged. "Bitch, are you hurt? That wolf jumped at you." She stood then checked over my body.

Jorie came over, sat next to me, then pulled Mikayla down to sit next to her. I could tell that Jorie was upset, but she was calmer than me and Mikayla. With Jorie already being a member of the tribe and pack, she was privy to information that me and my best friend were not. At the conclusion of this ceremony, we would have been official members of the tribe.

"I'm sorry that this happened," Jorie apologized. When I asked her who the wolf was, she huffed. "It was Patrick Lourie."

"Wow! I guess he was serious that it would be over his dead body that Thaddeus and I have our mating ceremony," I said. This situation wasn't funny, but how could I not laugh from crying any harder. *My fiancé's father just tried to kill me.*

Rummie stood off to the side with Claire who consoled

her. I wanted to go over and check on Rummie, but what could I say. *Hey, why'd your dad try to kill me?* We sat there forever. Mikayla and I didn't have the telepathic ability to talk to the pack, but I knew from certain moments that Jorie got quiet or walked away that she was communicating with the pack.

From what I understood, only people in a pack could communicate telepathically with each other. Claire was not a part of Thaddeus's pack, but her pack members were here. It was obvious that she was communicating with them.

After a while, a few more women from the tribe came into the building. They came over to us telling us that we should eat. I stood up. "I don't want to eat. I want Thaddeus. Where is my mate?" The second my question finished, it dawned on me that we hadn't completed the ceremony. Technically, Thaddeus was not my mate.

I turned to Mikayla. "We didn't finish the ceremony. Does that mean that they aren't our mates?" I asked her as if she had the tribal handbook. I covered my face with my hands, then cried into them. All of this bullshit and I still didn't have a mate. "I just want Thaddeus," I mumbled.

Arms wrapped tightly around me. A calm came over me. "He's coming, sis. I promise, he's coming."

I learned some time ago that Rummie's special gift was emotion control by touch. She had the ability to calm a person with a simple touch. When she first told me and Mikayla about her gift, I didn't understand the relevance of it. In this moment, at this time, I understood it fully because I needed it.

Thaddeus

Moments Before the Attack...

I couldn't keep my eyes off Elsbeth. She was gorgeously dressed in the tribal, ceremonial dress. When she walked toward me earlier, I had to give my dick a pep talk to not embarrass me in front of all these people.

My cousins from Washington State flew in to attend the mating ceremony. I was excited to see my male cousins Mason Senior and Junior, Kyle Senior and Junior, and my female cousin Willow. When I called Mason Sr. to tell him about what was going on, he didn't hesitate to be the officiant of the mating ceremony. He told me stories about my father when he was younger and his hatred toward mixed blood members of the pack.

Mason went a step further and brought his chief down with him so that we could spend some time together. He wanted me to have a conversation with Arrow about my decision of whether I would accept the counsels' decision to become the new chief. After the incident at Chepi's house, the council decided to have a meeting about my father's conduct. It was determined that he had many violations, some of which I was not privy to, that they thought it was best to remove him from his seat as chief. My father was not pleased; therefore, he chose to segregate from the pack.

Once segregated from the pack and Chepi told him to kick rocks, my father left the reservation all together. Chepi left soon after. Ahote, my father's spiritual advisor, once thought like my father when it came to wanting a pure bloodline for his family. That thought changed quickly after the counsels' ruling. He came to me, my mother, and sister to apologize for his involvement with the engagement fiasco. Enola, on the other hand, was still in her feelings for whatever reason. That blew me because she was still fucking with her very black, non-wolf man.

"The bond between mates is a sacred covenant that is blessed by the gods," Mason Sr. said. "You have been bound with the love of the gods and now we will..." He stopped talking before he straightened his back.

His action was one of his beast. We didn't have to be in the same pack to understand beast behavior. *"Someone is lurking in the woods."* I spoke telepathically with my pack.

The hairs on the back of my neck rose before I made eye contact with my mother. The cover of the night hid the physical presence of evil, but you can never hide evil from pure spirits. "Get them out of here!" I yelled.

Rummie grabbed Elsbeth's arm and pulled her back. Jorie snatched Mikayla back. My sister pulled my mate back just in time to prevent my father's wolf from pouncing on her. My mother shifted before I did and lunged at my father. Once I was shifted, I ran to join the fight.

"Get back!" my mother demanded. *"No one intervene!"* She and my father were fighting. Although she appeared to be winning, I still didn't like that she was fighting.

I moved to step in anyway but was stopped by Mason and Kyle Sr. stepping in front of me in their centaur beast form. "Do not intervene! This is between your mother and her mate!" Mason spoke out loud. We were cousins but we were not members of the same pack, so we could not communicate telepathically.

My father could not telepathically communicate with the pack, but he could with my mother because technically they were still mates and bounded. I'm not sure what my mother did, but my father's beast cried out. I rushed over with fear and worry coursing through my veins. My father's beast was lying on the ground with a horrific neck wound and my mother stood over him with a bloodied face. The sadness of her spirit couldn't be missed even in her beast form.

"Patrick, it didn't have to go this way." My mother's voice came out breathy in its telepathic form. "I told you that you were running out of chances when it came to messing with my babies."

The conversation that my mother had with my dying father was one-sided from my standpoint since I could only hear her. I wanted badly to hear what my father said. When she yelled that my mate was her baby too, I knew he more than likely attempted to separate Elsbeth's connection from my mother.

"I loved you, Patrick, I did. Our son told you that if you ever came for his mate that he would kill you," my mother said solemnly. "I would never allow my son to have that weight on his chest. I, however, will take all the weight of your death being because of my teeth." There was a pregnant pause before her beast leaned over my father's body. "Rest in hell, Patrick. You're no longer needed here."

My mother turned her back on my father, then shifted

back into her human form. She never cared for shifting into her beast unless it was necessary. One of the tribe women ran over to her with fabric to cover her body quickly. Once my mother was covered, she instructed me, Sabastian, and Farad to shift and get cleaned up.. I rushed to follow her instructions because I was ready to see my mate.

Those who were in their beast form started to shift into their human form. The ones who hadn't shifted left to retrieve coverings for those who were going to shift back to human form. I heard about Mason and Kyle Sr. having a centaur beast, but it was a completely different thing to see it. They were enormous!

My mother told the women to come to her house and the men were to come to mine. I wanted to get to Elsbeth to make sure that she was all right. Our ceremony was stopped right before the bonding portions of it. "When you think we can finish the ceremony?" I asked Mason Sr. after the men got to my house.

"I think you should give it a couple of days," he responded. "We could always do a private bonding to complete the ceremony for you, Sabastian, and Farad." Mason Sr. was extremely sympathetic. "Let's get cleaned up, so you can check on your mate."

It took longer than I would have liked for us to get ourselves together to head over to the community center. The ceremony was held outside behind the building where a majority of the tribal ceremonies were held. I communicated with Rummie throughout the night to make sure that Beauty was all right. The women of the tribe forced her to eat and Rummie used her gift to soothe Beauty to sleep.

When the men that were at my house got to the community center, Mikayla and Jorie rushed over to their mates. My sister rushed over to me. "Elsbeth is sleeping in the office. I'm going to Mama's house."

I pivoted on the heel of my foot to change the direction to head to the office. The door was closed when I got to the office. After I gently opened it, I saw my love laying on the couch that was against the wall. She looked angelic yet exhausted as she slept. Beauty was a wild sleeper, and the couch was no match for her limbs. I dropped to my knees near the top of the couch where her head lay. My hand rubbed through her hair.

She groaned a little before her body shifted. Seconds later, her eyelids slowly opened. It took her a few blinks before her eyes bucked, and she abruptly sat up. "Baby, are you all right?" Her hands went to the sides of my face. She turned my head and examined me. "Do you need anything?" she asked with tears welling in the corners of her eyes.

"All I need is you, Beauty. Give me a kiss," I told her. She leaned forward and kissed my lips. "Are you all right?" After she told me that she was fine, I asked, "Do you still want to be my wife?"

Her head bucked back. "Why would you ask me that? Do you not want to marry me anymore?" Her tone was panicked. "You don't want me to be your mate?"

"Calm down, Beauty," I said with my hands on the sides of her face. I kissed her all over her face. "Stop talking crazy. You're already my mate."

Her head dropped. I cupped my finger under her chin to lift her head. With sadness in her eyes, she said, "We didn't finish the ceremony. Um, is Mama Parie all right?"

I hoped my mother was all right, but I didn't truly know

the answer. I tried to communicate with my mother earlier while the men were at my house getting cleaned up, but she closed herself off to me. "I haven't spoken with her yet. Did you eat something?"

She nodded her head. "I ate something earlier." She fidgeted with her fingers. "Can I talk to Mama Parie, please?"

"Rummie, Elsbeth wants to talk to Ma." Rummie left when we got here to go to our mother, so I figured that she could get her to talk to me. *"Can you ask her to reach out to me please?"*

Rummie quickly responded to let me know that they were on their way back to the center in about twenty minutes. I told Beauty that she was on her way over. I sat on the couch next to her and just held her in silence. We'd sit like this until my mother came.

Over forty minutes later there was a knock on the office door before it opened. My mother walked in. She wore a new tribal dress and looked like she hadn't just been in a major fight. "My babies, are you all ready to finish this ceremony?"

My head tilted and eyes tightened. I leaned forward in my seat after I removed my arm from around Beauty. "Ma, we don't have to finish it today. We can do it at another time."

Beauty nodded. "Mama Parie, we can wait. It's all right." She sniffled a little before she continued. "I'm so sorry that I caused all of this tro—"

My mother put her hand up, then told Elsbeth to hush. "I'm going to ask you both a few questions. The only answer acceptable will be yes or no. Are we clear?" She paused to make sure we understood.

"Do you two love each other?" After we both said yes,

she then asked, "Do you want to be each other's mates?" Again, we said yes. "Thank you for answering those questions. Now that the questioning portion of this evening has ended, we can move on. Get both of y'all asses up so we can get you two bonded." She moved toward the door, turned to us, then said, "I will not allow your father to take this day from you."

My mother had sacrificed so much just so that I could mate with the woman that I loved. Yes, my father was a grimy bitch, but he was still her mate. She made a decision that ultimately ended the life of her mate so that her children could be happy, respected, and loved properly.

I stood from the couch, turned, then extended my hand to Beauty. She took my hand so that I could pull her up. "Are you ready to get bonded?"

She kissed my lips before she nodded. Moments later, we were in the main room with everyone. They had already set the room up so that we could complete the ceremony. The ladies took Elsbeth, Mikayla, and Jorie into the other room to freshen up. Once the ladies were ready, we all took our places again.

My mother walked over to me and placed a hand on each side of my face before pulling my forehead down to hers. "You, Rummie, and Elsbeth are my babies. Yes, I loved your father but when he chose himself over his children, he poked the mama wolf." She pulled her forehead from mine. "You may see me cry from time to time, but always remember... When a wolf cries, you still see the wolf's teeth. This mama wolf bites," she concluded before she winked.

Epilogue

A Couple Years Later...

"**B**eauty, why are you out here?" Thaddeus came home from a meeting with the counsel to lie with his wife, but she wasn't in the house. He knew she wasn't at the pharmacy because Elsbeth was officially on her maternity leave. Mikayla ran the pharmacy solely until Elsbeth returned.

Elsbeth looked up where she kneeled on the ground with gardening gloves and a gardening tool in her hand. Mama Parie had taught Elsbeth how to garden and it was her peace during her pregnancy. "Baby, look at these." She held up a head of cabbage. "I'm going to cook this tonight."

Thaddeus held his head back to the sky to ask the gods for patience. His mate gave him hell on a daily with her wanting to be everywhere. When he trained his sight back on his wife, she held her hand up for him to help her from the ground. Once she was on her feet, he kissed her lips. "Beauty, if I don't want you to work, why would you think it was okay to have your ass kneeled down in this dirt?" He huffed, then

161

with a smile, said, "Baby, I don't even let you get on your knees to suck my dick right now."

Elsbeth smacked his arm with a laugh. "Thad! Why would you say that?" Her husband's mouth could be reckless at times. "Let's get in the house."

Thaddeus grabbed his wife's gardening basket with one hand and her hand with his other. They walked from the garden that was between their and Mama Parie's house. By the time they got onto the front porch, Rummie was coming out of her house. She had the glow of happiness all over her. "Hey, Sissy Pooh!" Elsbeth called out to her.

Rummie smiled at the sight of her brother and sister-in-law. Their love inspired her years ago to be open to love herself. She wasn't married yet, but she had love all over her now. "Hey, my two favorite people and cargo." She walked over to rub Elsbeth's protruding seven-month pregnant stomach.

"Rummie, I know you knew she was out there in that damn garden," her brother fussed. "What I tell y'all about letting her get down there with all that dirt and shit?" He'd given specific instructions to everyone in the tribe regarding his wife.

Rummie and Elsbeth rolled their eyes. "Chief Thad, I'on care what you tell them other folks. If my sis wants to garden, then she's going to garden. You think I'm going to hinder an opportunity to taste some good ass food?" She pushed his shoulder playfully.

"Thank you, Sis." Elsbeth gave Rummie her cheeky smile. "Where you going?"

Rummie shook her head. "Nope, I'm about to go mind my business just like y'all should be doing." It annoyed her how much her business was suddenly the topic of discussion.

"You better tell that business that he needs to be making

his way here sooner than later," Thaddeus sternly said. He knew that his sister had a man and had one for a while. "Make sure you tell your business that shit."

He knew exactly who her man was due to his superb tracking skills. Thaddeus knew that his sister's beau was not a wolf, but now that didn't matter. As the chief, he made it clear that anyone that benefited the tribe was welcome regardless of their wolf/non-wolf status. Why Rummie made the decision to hide her man was a puzzle to him.

Rummie's hand went to her hip. "Thaddeus, if you want to practice parenting someone, you better carry your ass to Sabastian and Mikayla house to play with their kids." Sabastian and Mikayla added a baby girl to their family a year ago. She cut her eyes at her brother. "Reminder, our fuck ass daddy is dead."

Years ago, when their mother was forced to kill their father to protect their family, Rummie battled with her emotions about it. She loved her father dearly, but she would never pretend as if she was a daddy's girl. There had always been a wall between Rummie and her father that she never understood. After the incident at Chepi's house, the reality of the truth hit Rummie like a Mack truck. Her father couldn't love her because he didn't truly love himself. He was jaundiced by her chocolate skin complexion that matched his.

Thaddeus tittered. "All right, big sis. Just watch yourself." They hugged, then Elsbeth hugged her sister-in-law and told her to be careful.

Elsbeth didn't have to inquire about Rummie's boo because she knew who he was. The joys of sisterhood. Thaddeus stayed on the porch until his sister's car was out of view. When he walked into his house, his mother stood in their kitchen with a cup of coffee. "Good morning, Ma. To what do we owe this honor for the first time today?"

Parie made several visits to her son and daughter-in-law's home a day. She still worked as the tribal doctor and midwife as well as being instrumental in the pharmacy opening that was now jointly run by Elsbeth and Mikayla. When Parie wasn't performing her doctorly duties, she was busying herself with her grandbabies. Although Thad's child wasn't born yet, she claimed Sabastian and Mikayla's two children as her grandbabies. Farad and Jorie had a ten-month-old set of twins that she also considered her grandbabies.

"Not too much attitude with me, little boy," Thad's mother said before she sipped from her cup of coffee. She put the cup down, walked over to her son, then kissed his cheek. "I'm here because your wife wanted me to come help her cook dinner for everyone."

His brow arched. "You said cook dinner for everyone. Who is everyone, Ma?"

Elsbeth pranced into the kitchen from the bathroom where she washed her hands. She looked at her husband and knew there was about to be a problem. Thaddeus treated her like a porcelain doll since they found out she was pregnant. He tried to have her stop working the week after even though she was only ten weeks pregnant. She shut it down for as long as she could. It was actually Mama Parie that rained on her parade a couple of months ago when she told her that she needed to sit down because of blood pressure and blood sugar issues.

Thaddeus walked over to his wife. He admired the changes of her body that his son caused. Thaddeus decided that his son could have whatever he wanted, whenever he wanted, after the boost in Elsbeth's clinginess. He loved his wife to cling to him and his beast loved it more. "Beauty, who are we having over for dinner tonight?"

This had become a biweekly thing for Elsbeth. Her husband wouldn't mind these dinners if his wife didn't insist on doing all of the cooking. "Um, it's just going to be the usual," she responded innocently.

"Beauty, the usual could be anywhere from eight to twelve people," Thad pointed out. "Tell me which usual I should be prepared for."

His wife used her fingers to name and count the usual people. Her parents were coming to dinner, and he knew that would make her very happy. Harry and Marci still permanently lived in Raleigh; however, they spent a lot of time in Lumberton since Elsbeth's pregnancy. Thaddeus had toyed with the idea of asking them if they'd like to move into a house on the reservation.

After Chepi left the reservation, Parie purchased her home and used it as an Airbnb. The house was peculiarly built on the edge of the reservation which was about ten minutes away from Thaddeus and Elsbeth's home. Thad had mentioned the idea to his wife, but she was leery. She wanted to ensure that both the pack and her parents were safe. As the chief, Thaddeus could guarantee his in-laws protection.

"Elsbeth, after tonight's dinner, we are going to have someone else host them until after you have our son. Is that all right?" he asked. He saw the disappointment in her eyes. "No, don't do that. I didn't say that we couldn't have these dinners. I just want you to focus on relaxing."

With a tilted head and sad eyes, Elsbeth responded, "Okay, I'll relax. I asked Mama Parie to help me today."

Before he could respond, Mama Parie stepped to the side of her daughter-in-law. She looped her arm through Elsbeth's. "Can I have my daughter, so we can start dinner?"

Thaddeus kissed his wife's lips and his mother's fore-

head, then said, "Y'all got it. I'm about to go chop it up with Sabastian and Farad."

"I DON'T THINK THERE WILL BE AN ISSUE HAVING THEM move here.. Where the house is located, most of the tribe doesn't even consider it to be on the reservation. I do think you should have the conversation that needs to be had if they accept the invitation," Sabastian said before he took a pull from his blunt. Thaddeus and Sabastian discussed whether Elsbeth's parents should move on the reservation to be closer to their daughter.

When Thaddeus accepted the role of tribal chief, he was given the option like all chiefs to select his own spiritual advisor. That honor was bestowed upon Sabastian who accepted it with pride. Farad was promoted to the pack leader and Oscar was promoted to the second in the pack.

Thaddeus thought about what Sabastian said before he nodded. "I'll talk to Beauty about it." He took a pull from his blunt, exhaled the smoke, then snickered. "Let's move on to another topic. Did y'all get that invitation from Enola's ass?"

Farad burst into laughter. "Bro, I thought her ass accidentally sent that shit to my house. She's never fucked with me or Jorie for that matter, so I was confused as fuck."

Last week, Thaddeus received an invitation to a wedding. The envelope was addressed to just him and it just had a return address, but no name. Elsbeth checked their mailbox, so she intercepted it. When he got home from work at the Lumberton Post Office, his wife had the invitation and envelope on the fridge. When Thaddeus looked at the invitation, his wife simply said, "We should send a gift."

"Yeah, I got one too," Sabastian revealed. "I knew Enola

was on her good bullshit when I saw it. Hell, I'm just happy her ass moved the hell around."

That was something that Thaddeus was also grateful for. After Thaddeus and Elsbeth were mated, Enola was still in her feelings. For some reason she felt rejected, and she didn't like that. While everyone, including her father, had come to terms with the new normal, she suddenly had an issue. Once her father told her to grow up, she had a tantrum, then segregated from the pack. After several years, Enola decided that she now wanted to keep the bloodline pure. She was engaged to a Native American from another tribe who was not a wolf.

Thaddeus huffed. "Look, I'm just happy that I can look next to me every night and morning to see my mate, the woman that I love. I never thought I would have to lose my father to do it though."

Sabastian sat up straight in his seat with his stare on Thaddeus. "Well, let me ask you this. If I told you that I could turn back time and you had the option to course a different path, would you?"

The question was a loaded one, but an easy one to answer for Thaddeus. "I would take the same exact course that was taken before," he admitted. "Yeah, I lost my father, but was it really a loss? Patrick made it clear that there was no love to lose on his side when he attacked my mate, resulting in his mate killing him."

Farad shook his head. "Man, I didn't think your mom was going to be all right after that shit. Hell, sometimes I forget the shit happened because it's like it didn't even affect her."

"Oh, it affected her. I've heard her cries many nights."
Thaddeus and Elsbeth stayed with Mama Parie for almost a month after they were mated. They wanted to make sure that she was all right. In the light of day Mama Parie appeared to

be fine. It wasn't until the darkness of night that the pain tortured her.

Thaddeus smiled at the thought of his mother's strength. "Ma said that she would cry. She told me that the night we all were mated," he told his friends. "She also said crying wolves show teeth."

Sabastian smiled at the understanding of the statement. It was a statement that he'd heard her say since the incident. "Yeah, she says that shit all the time," he confirmed. He glanced at his chief. The man that he swore to guide to the best of his ability and the godfather of his children. "Bro, what does Mama Parie say about those teeth of hers though?"

They all guffawed for a moment. Mama Parie was hell, but she stood by everything she said, did, or thought. With a puffed-out chest, Thaddeus looked between his friends, then said, "Ma says those teeth bite." And damn, did they.

All Scootched In

About Author Mel Dau

Mel Dau 'Melvin's Daughter' has been taking the literary world by storm since April of 2018 with her debut release *A Charleston Love Story: Khiaere and Phy* where she highlighted her hometown Mount Pleasant, South Carolina. The first two years of her career she published fifteen titles under Queens of Lit Presents that all debuted in the top twenty-five on Amazon's Best Sellers Chart.

In 2020, this obsessive reader turned author had the privilege to sign to B. Love Publications where she continues to grow and sharpen her God given craft. Her first Best Seller came with her title *Pet the Kitty* in July of 2020. To further grow her empire, in August of 2020, she established Mel Dau Publications, LLC. Since, she has had great success with every release including adding audiobooks to her repertoire.

Through her writing she has set up a lane all her own, being the Queen of Informational Dramas. With each release she fulfills her purpose to her readers with her E^3 formula – to entertain, encourage, and educate. Her overall desire is to use her fiction catalog to help change at least one person's non-fiction reality.

Mel Dau is a proud member of Zeta Phi Beta Sorority, Incorporated and the mother of a young adult. In March of 2024, she took the leap of faith and made the pivot from an HR professional to a full-time author. Being an author is at the center of the purpose of her life.

Connect with Mel Dau

Mania Crew Email Subscription:
https://bit.ly/MelDauEmailManiaCrew

Website (Paperback Sales):
https://bit.ly/MelDauBookPills

Catalog (Amazon Links):
https://bit.ly/MelDauLinks

Facebook:
https://bit.ly/MelDauFB

Facebook Reader's Group (Mania Crew):
https://bit.ly/MelDauManiaCrewFBGroup

Instagram:
https://bit.ly/MelDauIG

Connect with Mel Dau

TikTok:
https://bit.ly/MelDauTikTok

Email:
Meldauspublications@gmail.com

Made in the USA
Monee, IL
01 March 2025

13174308R00105